Peter Reese Doyle

PUBLISHING

Colorado Springs, Colorado

AMBUSHED IN AFRICA

Copyright © 1993 by Peter Reese Doyle

Library of Congress Cataloging-in-Publication Data
Doyle, Peter Reese, 1930-
        Ambushed in Africa / Peter Reese Doyle.
        p. cm— (Daring Adventure Series)
        Summary: David Curtis, in Africa for a visit to his friends Mark
        and Penny Daring, helps them thwart attempts to steal the claim
        papers to a diamond field and to capture Penny as a hostage.
        ISBN 1-56179-142-3
        [1. Africa—fiction.] I. Title. II Series: Doyle, Peter Reese,
        1930- Daring Adventure Series.

Published by Focus on the Family Publishing, Colorado Springs,
Colorado, 80995

Edited by Etta Wilson
Cover illustration by Ken Spengler
Cover design by James A Lebbad

Printed in the United States of America

97 98/ 10 9 8 7

For

My daughter Susan

*Whose loving encouragement
inspired these tales.*

CONTENTS

CHAPTER 1

BACK IN AFRICA

British Airways Flight 537 broke through the thick clouds into the bright African sunlight just ten miles from the airport. David Curtis peered through the plane's thick plastic window at the scattered houses that littered the brown land on the outskirts of the city.

As the earth came closer, he noted the roads that converged on the metropolis like twisted broken spokes reaching for the hub of a wheel. The aircraft turned, the sun's rays flashed across the wing into his eyes, and he had to look away until the plane had completed the turn.

David had slept on the overnight flight from London. His lean six-foot-one frame was stiff from hours of sitting. His muscles practically screamed for exercise. He rubbed his eyes and tried to straighten his neatly trimmed hair.

Suddenly he realized how close they were to landing. He stuffed the book he'd been reading into his carryon pack and pushed it back under his seat. He hated to put away Herodotus's history at this point. The ancient saga of the thirteen thousand embattled Greek soldiers had gripped his attention for hours, and he wanted to

1

know how they would escape the encircling Persian armies.

The plane was banking for its final approach, and his thoughts turned to the friends he would soon be seeing. Mr. Daring had written that he would meet him at the airport when he arrived; David wondered—not for the first time—if both Mark and Penny would be there too.

Mark and David were both seventeen, Penny a year younger, and they'd known each other for years. Their parents were close friends. Mr. Daring and David's father had worked for the same mining engineering firm before the Darings moved to East Africa. Since that time, the two families had exchanged visits. This was not David's first time in Africa, and his pulse quickened at the prospect of being back on that exciting continent.

Suddenly he felt the plane jar as the wheels lowered for the landing. The pitch of the engines changed, almost hurting his ears, the wing flaps came back and down, and David's stomach tightened with excitement as the big jet hurtled toward the field.

Houses flashed past the window in a blur. David saw the edge of the runway just before they touched down. He was sweating now, as the heat from the ground air warmed the inside of the plane faster than the air conditioning could handle it. From the front seats in his section, David could hear babies crying as the increased pressure of the cabin hurt their ears.

Then the wheels touched; once, twice, and they were on the ground, rushing past the terminal at great speed. The big plane slowed gradually, made its turn, and began to taxi toward the terminal. Finally, the engines stopped.

What a relief to stand again! David stretched, picked up the carryon bag from under the seat, and joined the line of eager passengers moving to the door. Europeans, Africans, British, Asians, and Americans were speaking to each other in a dozen different languages, all happy to be on land. He followed the crowd off the plane and into the terminal where customs officers inspected their baggage.

Finally, he was through customs! Carrying his luggage he went into the waiting room of the noisy terminal, eyes searching eagerly for his friends among the crowds of people from different lands.

Then he heard Mark's shout. "David! Over here!"

And there they were: Mr. Daring, Mark, and Penny! David hurried through the gate to meet them.

Mark was blond and even more powerfully muscled than he had been the last time David saw him. Beside him stood Penny, slender in a light blue dress, looking prettier than he'd even remembered. David's heart skipped a few beats. Mr. Daring grinned with pleasure as David approached.

Mark reached him first. He gripped David's hand, and both boys laughed as they tested each other's strength—as they always did. And, as always, they were even! Mark's open face showed his surprise. He never understood how someone as lean as David could have a grip as strong as his own.

"Let him go, Mark," Penny said, and she threw her arms around David's neck. He hugged her briefly, then quickly let go, his face red. She laughed up at him. "Oh! We're so glad to see you again, David! Living here in Africa we miss our friends from home—especially you." Her light brown hair was tied away from her face with a blue ribbon the same color as her dress. He couldn't think of anything to say to her, so he just grinned. Then he tore his eyes away to greet her father.

Mark had gotten his size from his father; Mr. Daring was also blond, powerfully built. He was obviously very fit. "Welcome back, David," he said as he pumped David's hand with obvious pleasure, blue eyes sparkling in his wide, tanned face. He'd always regarded David as another son.

Then he picked up one of David's bags, Mark got the other, and they moved rapidly out of the terminal toward the parking lot. Penny held David's arm as they followed her father and brother, asking questions about his family and his flight. One question followed another so quickly that they arrived at the Darings' car before he realized they'd left the terminal!

Suddenly Mr. Daring stopped. "Mark!" he said. "Those are the men I told you about." He was looking back toward the terminal.

The three teenagers turned in time to see two men

enter a cab. One was lean, of medium size, with blond hair. The other was dark and massive.

"The medium-sized one is Hoffmann and the other is Walther," Mr. Daring said grimly. "Colonel Lamumba warned us that they were returning."

"Who are they, Dad?" Penny asked, as the cab drove rapidly away, turned a corner, and disappeared behind the airport terminal.

"They call themselves mining engineers," Mr. Daring replied, "but they're known to be involved in some kind of dirty work in the diamond fields. A friend in the army warned me about them. I've known about them for the past two years. Just remember what they look like."

Then he changed the subject. "But David's on vacation! We won't worry about those men. Get in the car and we'll go to our plane."

After putting David's bags in the trunk, they took off. Mr. Daring drove them past several hangars until they came to the area where private and corporate aircraft were kept. He stopped the car in front of a small hangar before which a green-trimmed white Cessna was parked. Two mechanics were checking it out.

"Ready to fly again?" Mr. Daring asked David as they all got out of the car. David tried not to grimace and his friends laughed. Mr. Daring and Mark took some boxes from the trunk of the car and put them in the waiting Cessna along with David's suitcases. Then, while Mr. Daring checked the plane with the mechanics, the

the three teenagers talked as fast as they could, trying to catch up on each other's activities during the past year.

While they talked, David kept looking at the vast blue sky and filling his lungs with warm fresh air. And the colors! Everywhere he looked there was color— bright clothing on the women in the terminal, bright paint on the private hangars and planes, bright bill-boards with garish red and yellow and black advertisements. A riot of color struck his eyes.

And the sounds! Giant jets filled the air with their roar as they landed and took off regularly from the international airport. David felt like a bird released from a cage!

"Boy, was it cramped on that plane! I need exercise!" he said as he stretched his arms.

"You'll get plenty of that," Mark laughed. "Dad's got us on a real schedule—I mean, a real schedule! We run, pump iron, and Matt, his radio man, trains us in karate four times a week. We'll work some of that fat off you in no time! You might even get a muscle or two!" Mark's broad face beamed at his friend.

"That's ridiculous!" Penny protested. "David hasn't got any fat on him. Look who's talking." She poked her brother's flat stomach.

"Hey, what do you mean? I'm all muscle." It was true. His father had definite ideas about physical fit-ness, and Mark's strength and physical conditioning proved it.

"Let's go!" Mr. Daring called as he opened the passenger door to the Cessna. "The plane's ready. You two get in back." He gestured toward Mark and David.

"Come on, David." Mark climbed in and went to a back seat. David followed, not liiking forward to being cooped up again, but glad that this was the last leg of his long journey. As he climbed in back, he relished again the familiar smells of an airplane cockpit—oil and leather, electrical equipment and grease. Penny and her father got in front, and they all buckled their seat belts.

Mr. Daring began to go through the flight check. Then he started the engine and called the tower.

Mark spoke above the roar of the engine. "We'll get to fly a lot, David. I take mail to several of the mission stations, as well as to Dad's mining teams. And there're some new people I want you to meet."

"You mean girls, don't you, Mark?" Penny interrupted, looking back from the seat beside her father. "I know why you volunteered to fly to those missions." Her brown eyes crinkled as she teased her brother.

"Don't be ridiculous," Mark retorted with an air of wounded innocence. "I just like to help out. That's all."

Then her father gunned the engine and talking became difficult. Mr. Daring started the Cessna rolling toward the runway, checking instruments as they taxied along. He spoke to the tower and finally, they were cleared for takeoff.

This was the part of flying David loved the most—tearing down the runway, the light plane bouncing slightly, the roar of the engine filling his head, hangars and planes flashing by, blue sky beckoning as the craft gains power and speed; then the liftoff—the sense of release from the ground below! Every takeoff thrilled him as much as the one before.

They were climbing steeply. Mr. Daring turned the plane toward the brown mountains that shimmered through the distant haze. The Cessna climbed steadily as it headed inland, cleaving the sky like an arrow in flight and leaving the airport behind. To their left, huge cumulus clouds towered thousands of feet into the sky.

Mark read during most of the trip, but David kept looking out the windows, relishing every new sight below. Penny dozed. She'd seen it all before. Then the two-hour flight was over and they began to descend.

David felt his ears pop as the craft lost altitude. Mark pointed past him to the buildings below. "There's our pool. How about a swim?"

"Great!" David replied.

Looking down, he saw a dozen houses, several office buildings, storage sheds and garages, and a hangar for the planes. A radio tower pierced the sky between the storage shed and the hangar. Two Land Rovers, several pickups, and three sedans were parked beside the buildings. It had been two years since David's last visit, but he had not forgotten this place.

The plane landed swiftly and smoothly, turned at the end of the runway, and taxied back to the hangar. Several people were waiting for them, and David recognized Penny and David's mother, Carolyn Daring, and their younger brother, Benjamin, and sister, Ruth.

David's heart was pounding with excitement as he got out of the plane. He was back in Africa! Wonderful, wonderful Africa!

CHAPTER 2

THEY'VE KIDNAPPED MR. RUSH!

Mark woke David the next day with a blow to his pillow. "Time for exercise, you lazy bum," he said.

David rolled out of bed and tossed his own pillow, but Mark dodged.

"I'll get you later," David laughed.

They quickly pulled on shorts, shirts, and running shoes. Then David followed Mark out the front door where they joined Mr. Daring in the yard. Mr. Daring led them in warm-up exercises for about ten minutes. Then they walked down the drive to the engineering lab, where Mr. Daring began to jog. The boys followed after him.

They ran past the buildings and down the road. Tall trees loomed ahead, and beyond these, the distant mountains shimmered in the morning haze. Soon they left the boundaries of the mining station. The path led through tall, dark green grass, forcing them to run single file. They were sweating now although the air was not yet hot.

As they ran, David wondered if there were animals lurking in the grass, waiting to pounce! He noticed the pistol strapped to a holster on Mr. Daring's belt.

"What's the gun for, Mr. Daring?" David asked, just a bit breathlessly.

"Wild pigs, David," Mark's dad replied. "Sometimes they roam this area. We always take a gun with us when we leave the station. Have you kept up your shooting?"

"Yes, sir, Dad and I shoot a lot. He's got a friend on the police force who's trained us in combat shooting."

"Fine," Mr. Daring replied. "Mark and Penny are good shots too. We'll do some target shooting while you're here."

Mr. Daring suddenly took a path that branched to the left, and the boys followed him. Now they were running under a grove of trees, the thick bush making a wall on both sides. Their path twisted and turned, and soon David lost all sense of direction—they'd never taken him this way before. The cries of birds sounded from the bush on each side of them, and once he thought he heard monkeys as well.

Half an hour later David realized they'd made a big circle, for as they left the woods, they came in sight of the mining station's buildings.

Back in the house, they showered and dressed. The two had just picked up their Bibles when Mrs. Daring called them to breakfast.

Ruth, who was ten, and Benjamin, seven, were waiting for them. They could hardly wait to talk with David again. But Mrs. Daring insisted that they let the boys eat first.

That's when David realized that he was starving! He and Mark ate as much as the rest combined. When Penny commented on this, David told her that he was eating all her mother had cooked so as not to hurt her feelings.

Penny laughed. "You're such a gentleman, David, and *so* considerate of my Mom."

David noticed a dimple in her cheek when she smiled. "I can't help it," he admitted with a grin. "It's the way I was raised." He turned to Ruth. "Would you pass me the muffins again, please?"

They all laughed and passed him muffins, butter, milk—and everything else that was on the table.

When it seemed David was about finished Mr. Daring stood up. "Mark, bring David to the office when you both are finished, and I'll show him the mining operation. He can work with you and Don Ferguson for the first few days."

He looked at his wife. "Thanks for breakfast, honey," he told her as he excused himself and headed for the office. They all got up then, and everybody pitched in to clear the table.

A short while later the two boys were in the office of Don Ferguson, a short, compact man from Minnesota. Mr. Ferguson was the head engineer and had worked for Mark's dad in the mining industry for many years. He and David remembered each other from David's previous visit. Mark left to work on a project he'd been assigned by his dad, while Mr. Ferguson showed David the offices and labs. As they went through the buildings, he explained to David the work that went on in each place. David found this fascinating—he'd not seen all this on his past visit.

Then Mr. Ferguson took him to Mr. Daring's office. Mark's dad waved him to a chair beside his desk and told him the history of the station. He had started it seven years before, doing work for various businesses and for the government as well.

"They send mineral samples for us to analyze," he explained. "They also ask our people to visit different places and evaluate the mineral prospects for them. The people who work for us are from several different countries—and continents. It's a great team and we're proud of them."

He reached for his phone, pressed a button, and, when Mark answered, asked him to come for David.

David spent the rest of the morning with Mark, who explained the various kinds of reports on diamond mining he was preparing. David was intrigued; the more he read, the more interesting the work became. Later, Mark dictated summaries of some of the reports while David typed them into the computer for him. The boys worked at the office until noon.

"Time for a swim, David. Let's go," Mark announced

and stood to stretch.

They went home, changed, and plunged into the pool. Ruth and Benjamin were there as well as several neighbor kids. Mark, David, and Penny had a real work-out tossing a ball with the smaller children, chasing and being chased. By lunchtime they were starving again.

"Where's Dad?" Mark asked his mom as he helped himself to another sandwich.

"He called to say he would be working and asked if you and David would bring his lunch to his office when you were through," she answered. Mrs. Daring was a tall, cheerful woman with light brown hair like her daughter's. She loved to tease Mark and David as much as Penny did.

When the two boys arrived with Mr. Daring's lunch, they found him working at his desk.

"Close the door, boys, and sit while I eat and tell you what I've *just* learned." Mark and David sensed that something serious was up.

They were right. The engineer paused a moment, looking gravely at the boys. He chose his words carefully.

"David, Tom Rush is an engineer at our station in Mboto up in the hills. He's working on an important project for us, and he has two technicians helping him. An hour ago he called by radio. He used a code word we'd agreed on in case an emergency arose. Then he said he had some research ready and asked if I wanted to send a plane for it, or have him bring it with him when he returns tomorrow. This was his way of telling me I should come get him by plane—in a hurry!" Mr. Daring paused and began to eat one of the sandwiches they'd brought him.

"I told him the plane is already scheduled to go up-country this afternoon and could easily swing by and pick up his report. I asked when it would be ready." Mr. Daring frowned. "What I really wanted to know was how quickly he wanted me to come get him."

Daring ate more of the sandwich and looked soberly at Mark and David. They were all ears, sensing that this was serious business.

"Rush told me he would have it all together in a couple of hours. Around three o'clock or so," he said. "He made it sound casual, but I knew that was exactly when he wanted to be picked up. So I told him the plane would be there sometime after three—just to keep it relaxed in case the wrong people were listening in on our radio.

"Rush didn't give the code for *immediate* danger, so Mark, I want you and David to fly to Mboto, pick Tom up, and bring him back here. It's a forty-minute flight. The plane's all checked and ready, the weather's fine, and the men at the hangar have made out your flight plan. But first go back to the house for your survival pack, and make up one for David. I need to wait for a very important message from another of our men."

"That's great!" Mark said enthusiastically. "We're on our way!" His broad face beamed with pleasure as he led David from his father's office.

The two ran for the house. There Mark filled two canteens and gave one to David. He also checked to see that he had first aid equipment, an extra gallon of water, flashlights, and ammunition for the .357 revolver his father kept in the plane.

"We always take this survival stuff with us when we travel," Mark explained to David. "People have lost their lives just because they thought they wouldn't need food or water on short flights like this. But it can take a long time to find a little plane that crashes in the thick brush, so we don't take any chances."

"Makes sense to me," David agreed. "Besides, I get hungry and thirsty real often!" Both boys laughed.

They met Mark's dad at the hangar. The mechanic had brought out the smaller four-passenger aircraft. "It's ready, Jim," he told Mr. Daring.

"Let's see the plane's emergency kit," Mr. Daring said. They checked it and found more supplies, flashlights, water, and flares. Mr. Daring and the boys then studied the flight plan.

"You're familiar with the landing strip beside the station, Mark. Just land, pick up Rush, and head back right away. And both of you keep your eyes open for the two men we saw at the airport yesterday. I just have a feeling about them."

"Yes, sir," Mark said eagerly.

"Let's pray for a safe trip, then," his dad said. The three of them stood beside the cockpit door with their arms joined while Mr. Daring asked for the Lord's protection on their flight. When he finished, he stepped back from the door. He couldn't help grinning at their excitement.

Mark and David climbed aboard and strapped themselves in the seats. Mark started the engine, then signalled the mechanics to remove the chocks from the wheels. He taxied the plane out to the end of the runway and went through his final check. The plane shook as the noise of the engine swelled. Mark cut the power, released the brake, and began to move forward. Gradually he increased throttle and the craft picked up speed. Then they were off the ground, climbing for altitude.

David studied the terrain over which they flew as they headed toward the mountains, looming dark and ominous in the distance. He turned to Mark and spoke over the noise of the engine. "You promised me adventure, but I didn't think it would happen this soon!"

"Neither did I," Mark grinned. "I don't know much about the work at Mboto station—Dad's kept pretty quiet about it."

He adjusted the trim of the plane as they continued their gradual climb; then he began to point out landmarks. "You'll get to know the area soon," he added. "We fly four or five times a week so you'll have lots of practice."

The time passed quickly. Suddenly Mark pointed out the forward window. "There it is—Mboto. We'll fly south of the town and then approach the station from the west so we don't advertise ourselves more than necessary in case there is something strange going on down there."

They passed the town, and Mark turned the plane toward the station. "That's it," he pointed.

David saw a small building and the airstrip beside it. A station wagon was parked in front.

As they began to descend, he noticed a cloud of dust racing along the road that led north from the station. A car was moving fast, going up a winding road away from the mining office and hurtling toward the foothills at tremendous speed. The dust from the speeding car climbed above the tall trees on either side of the road as it charged ahead. David pointed to the car and turned to Mark. "That guy's moving almost as fast as we are!" he said.

Mark studied the vehicle for a moment. "He sure is," he agreed, "but he's taking a chance on that road. It's rough and it's narrow."

"Is he leaving the mining station?" David asked. "The road seems to go right past the building we're headed for."

"I think you're right, David." Mark was frowning.

"Maybe we should follow him a little way," David suggested.

Mark didn't say anything as he thought this over, and David didn't push him, knowing he'd had his orders from his dad.

"Let's do it!" Mark had made up his mind. "We've got a few minutes to spare, but this plane is too suspicious. We'll drop lower and stay behind those hills to his left, so he can't see us." Mark banked into a left turn, descending as he went and putting the range of hills between the plane and the car.

"Why would a car be racing away from the station when we're coming to pick up Mr. Rush?" he asked. He piloted the plane even lower so that they flew just above the tops of the tall trees on the hills below. They could keep the craft out of sight of the racing car which was still a couple of miles ahead of them.

"He won't hear us over the noise of his car," Mark said, "and we can weave back and forth so we don't get ahead of him. I'd like to see what he's up to before we go back for Mr. Rush."

"Should we radio your father about this?" David asked.

Mark thought for a minute. "Maybe we better not. If people are listening in on Dad's radio, we might tip them off. Mr. Rush can call from the station using the special radio code if he needs to."

For several minutes they shadowed the car, flying quite far behind, twice turning in a complete circle so as not to get too close to their quarry.

Suddenly the car left the road, turned sharply, and headed directly into steeper hills, going up a very narrow trail.

Mark looked puzzled. Suddenly he exclaimed,

"I've got it! They're heading up a track that dead-ends on Wild Boar Hill. There's no other way out—not for a car. I bet they're going to hide in a shed we built there several years ago. We haven't used it for a year, and it's a great place to hide. You can't be seen from the road or from the air, because the trees and the bush are too thick. That's it! That's where they're going!" He was excited now. "Let's get back to the station."

He turned the plane and eased the throttle forward for more speed. Soon they were above the airstrip that went alongside two small buildings of the mining station. Mark circled once, then turned to land. "Oh, oh! Something's wrong down there," he said. He was frowning.

"What is it?" David asked.

"The men always come out when we fly in. I don't see anybody." He was clearly puzzled as he brought the craft down.

The landing strip was narrow, but the grass-covered surface was very smooth. Mark landed skillfully, turned, and taxied back to the white-painted buildings. While Mark studied the strip ahead, David watched the two buildings. Still no one appeared.

Mark stopped the plane, locked the brakes, and cut the engine. His face was troubled as he undid his seatbelt. "Let's go!" he said. "Something's wrong!"

The boys piled out of the plane and rushed toward the office. David got there first, yanked open the door, and raced inside. Mark was right behind.

The place was a shambles! Papers covered the floor, files were overturned, two chairs were on their sides, pictures and maps had been yanked roughly off the wall and thrown to the floor. No one was in sight.

Mark ran back to the inner office and jerked open the door. And there, sitting against the wall, bound hand and foot, gagged and mad as they could be, were the two technicians! Mr. Rush was nowhere to be seen!

CHAPTER 3

CHAOS

Mark yanked his knife from his pocket, knelt by the larger of the two men, and began to cut the ropes that bound his arms behind his back. David pulled out his knife and cut loose the other man.

"What happened here, Mr. Sanderson?" Mark asked, as he sliced the last rope.

Sanderson was outraged. Rubbing his swollen ankles and wrists, he glanced at David. "Who's your friend?" he asked Mark.

"That's David Curtis," Mark replied. "He's just come from the States."

"We're glad to see you both," Sanderson said gratefully. "This is Mike Wilcox, David."

Wilcox, like Sanderson, still sat on the floor, wincing with pain as the blood rushed back to his hands and feet. His dark hair contrasted sharply with his pale face.

"Two men with pistols rushed us a while ago," Ed Sanderson explained. "We had no warning at all. They shoved us into this room, tied us up, and locked us in. Then we heard them asking Tom for the report he'd written for your dad. He'd finished it earlier

22

today." Suddenly Sanderson choked. "I need some water," he said, looking toward the watercooler in the corner.

David rushed over, found cups beside the cooler, and brought water to both men.

Sanderson continued his story. "Tom told them the report was in his briefcase on the desk. Then we heard them tearing up the room searching for other things. They made Tom go with them—and that's all we know."

Both men struggled to their feet and stumbled weakly into the large front office with the boys following. There the two technicians pulled some chairs upright and collapsed into them, shaking their heads at the mess that surrounded them.

"We heard them leave," Wilcox said. "The tires were screeching as they turned around and tore down the road." His plump face was as angry as Sanderson's. Then he thought of something else. "Tom had a message earlier, just before he called your dad."

"What kind of message?" Mark asked quickly.

"Some kind of warning," Wilcox answered. "He didn't tell us what he'd heard, only that we should start packing while he finished writing his report. He said we'd all have to leave, that he'd go by plane, and we'd drive out. But those guys got here first."

"He thought we'd have more time, I think," Sanderson said, "but he didn't tell us anything more about it."

"Then the men who got Mr. Rush got his report too!" Mark's concern showed in his face.

"Well, they got Rush—but they didn't get his report," Sanderson said. He chuckled, as he continued to rub his legs and wrists. The boys looked at him in surprise.

"Tom fooled them. I saw him shove the report under a mat on his desk just as the men charged through the door. He sure thought fast! He told them his report was in his case, but it wasn't. And it's still here under that map of the mine."

Sanderson struggled to his feet and went over to Rush's desk, the only one still standing upright. He rummaged through a pile of papers. "Here it is!" he said triumphantly, holding up several pages which were stapled together.

"Great" Mark said. But it didn't solve the problem of Mr. Rush's kidnapping. "We've got to get Mr. Rush back," Mark said anxiously. "We think we know where they've taken him." He told the men about the car he and David had seen racing up the mountain road to the shed.

"Let's call your dad," Sanderson suggested.

"Just be careful what you say," David volunteered. "Mr. Daring told us Mr. Rush used a code on the radio, so other people may be listening in on your communications. Why not just tell him that Mr. Rush has been taken, and that he should call the police right away? When they get here, we can tell them about the cabin. We don't want to tip off the kidnappers."

But then David had another idea. "Mark! We could fly over that road and keep an eye on the shed while the men drive back with Mr. Rush's report."

"Fine!" Mike Wilcox said, deciding the matter for him. "We'll take the report to your dad, and he can get help up here for Tom. Ed, call Mr. Daring while I get some things together and close the place down."

Sanderson went to the radio and called in the message while Wilcox packed up papers and personal things. Mark and David used the moments to straighten up some of the mess in the room.

Sanderson finished the call and looked anxiously at Mark. "Your dad said to tell you boys not to get in any trouble. Just let the police handle this."

Mark grinned. "We'll be careful! We can stay in the air and watch the road. If those kidnappers leave the shed we'll see which way they're going. We'll radio Dad and he can tell the police. Those guys will be trapped!"

"Let's go, Ed," Wilcox said. As soon as they were out, he locked the building. Then the two men got in the car, waved to Mark and David, and headed toward Mboto and the station.

Mark and David ran to the plane and climbed in. Mark started the engine, taxied to the end of the strip, tested the power, then roared down the field and took to the air.

Once aloft, Mark turned the plane and followed the road the kidnappers had taken. The ground beneath

them was very hilly. He kept the Cessna low and
behind hills, hoping to shield the sound from the men
in the cabin as they came nearer.

"We've got to stay within sight of the road where
that track to the cabin branches off," he said to David,
speaking loudly over the engine's noise. "Then if they
drive off, we'll see their dust and call Dad."

Soon they saw where the narrow car track—really
just a rough path—left the road. Mark turned the plane
away in a wide curve, dipping below the hilltops to
stay out of sight. The ground below was hidden
beneath the thick green foliage of low bush and tall
trees. Mark and David had to watch for the car track as
they flew.

"Look!" David said suddenly. He pointed to the
ground ahead and to their left on the other side of the
range of hills.

Mark dipped the nose down and looked where
David pointed. At once he saw another road going the
same direction as the one they were watching.

"Can you land on that road, Mark?" David asked.
"We could climb that hill and get a look at the cabin
from there."

Mark raised his eyebrows. "I don't know. I've never
landed on a road before. It looks rough." More cautious,
less impulsive than his friend, Mark considered David's
idea.

"We've got wide tires for rough ground," David
urged.

"Well, let's take a look," Mark replied. Banking the Cessna, he crossed the hills, then dropped lower so they could study the road David had pointed out. Soon they were close to the tall trees below and could see patches of rocky ground between the branches. Mark hoped that the hills between the plane and the cabin would mask the noise of their engine. Both boys studied the road as the Cessna glided slowly above it.

"I think we can do it!" Mark said. "It'll be rough, but it looks O.K. Then we can hide the plane under some of those tall trees while we scout the cabin. I'll fly over once again so we can pick the right place. Hold on."

David kept silent as Mark pulled the craft around in a tight turn, circled, and came back. They studied the ground carefully. Suddenly David pointed down. "There! We could put the plane there, behind that group of trees, so it won't be seen from the road!"

Mark looked it over as they passed. "That's it!" he said. "Let's go."

He flew a little farther and then, turning around again, came back over the road and dropped slowly to a landing. The plane bounced over the rough surface, rocking from side to side as the wide wheels absorbed much of the shock of the road's uneven surface. Mark began to apply the brakes, and they had a moment's panic before the aircraft slowed enough for Mark to turn onto the grass. He headed into the gap in the trees, then turned to his left. The plane bounced wildly as he guided it behind a clump of high bush. Here he cut the engine.

The sudden silence was deafening! Both were suddenly struck with the enormity of what they had decided to do. Neither said anything for a moment.

Then David grinned over at Mark in visible relief. "Great landing!"

"I'm not so sure," Mark replied, shaking his head. "Those bumps gave me a scare." He unstrapped his seat belt, and David did the same. They climbed out and stood by the plane, surveying the scene.

Mark looked at the trees that surrounded them on three sides. The plane was hidden from the road. Then he had an idea. "Let's turn the nose around, so we can get away in a hurry if we need to."

"Good idea," David agreed.

They went back to the tail, one on each side, and lifted together, turning the craft around and pointing it back the way they'd come in to land. "All we have to do now is start the engine and taxi around those trees to get on the road," Mark observed with satisfaction. "Then we can take off in a hurry."

They were sweating as they leaned against the plane and began to make their plans. David spoke first. "Remember, those guys have guns. We don't want to do anything stupid."

"You're right," Mark said. "We've got one too, but we sure don't want to have to use it. Besides," he added thoughtfully, "Penny would kill me if you got hurt in a shoot-out!"

David felt his face get red. "That's crazy," he replied.

"Hey! I almost forgot!" Mark said, straightening his powerful frame and looking back into the cockpit of the Cessna. "We've got a couple of cans of chemical mace in the plane. We carry them in case we meet wild dogs or animals we don't want to shoot."

He climbed back in the plane, rummaged around in a pack, and came out carrying the two cans. He gave one to David. "Know how these work?" he asked.

"I sure do," David replied. "Let's go!"

Turning their backs to the plane and the road, they began to climb, moving carefully through the grass between the tall trees. There were rocks all over the place, some visible, some hidden in the grass. It was cooler under the branches, but the humidity was greater. They were both sweating as they went up the steep and uneven incline.

"Watch for snakes," Mark said quietly as they skirted bushes and piles of loose rock.

They kept climbing until they reached the top of the hill. Here they paused to catch their breath and to study the ground that fell away before them. Patches of clear blue sky showed between the tree branches. They felt a slight breeze at this height, but the humidity was still oppressive.

Suddenly the silence of the woods was split by the raucous cries of angry birds to their left. Both boys jumped, startled. They had a strange sense that the place was closing in on them; it had a sinister feeling that made them uneasy.

"This place gives me the creeps!" David stepped back against a large tree.

"Me too," Mark agreed. "Let's go find that cabin. But be careful. They may have someone outside watching."

They began to climb down the steep incline, careful not to dislodge loose rocks that would tumble downhill and alarm the kidnappers. Cautiously they picked their way through clumps of thick bush, around tree trunks, over slabs and piles of rock. They scanned the terrain below as they descended.

David spoke quietly. "The cabin should be over there—I think." He pointed to their right.

"Let's keep track of some landmarks," Mark cautioned. "We wouldn't want to lose our way getting back—especially if we're in a hurry!"

"Right!" David agreed.

They'd gone about fifty yards when Mark grabbed David's arm and whispered, "There it is!" He pointed toward a thick clump of trees to their right. Through these they could see the side of the black car they'd followed earlier. Behind that they saw the faded brown wall of the wooden shed.

"That's it," Mark whispered with suppressed excitement. "There's only one door, and that faces away from us toward the road. But they might see us from the side windows. so we'll have to keep low when we move. We'd better make sure no one else is around— or a watchdog."

Crouched behind the large bush on the top of the

hill, Mark and David studied the ground below with great care. They picked out clumps of bushes behind which they could hide as they approached the building.

"Do I look as nervous as you do?" David asked quietly.

"I'm afraid so," Mark replied. Their shirts were wet with sweat from the humidity, nervousness, and exertion.

Suddenly they heard yells from the cabin! There was a loud crash, then more yells.

They ran to the shed behind the cabin and crouched low beside the wall. Again they heard the men inside yelling.

"I'll take a look," David said. He moved silently to the side window and peered carefully in. Mark crouched beside him.

One glance was enough! David bent down and whispered urgently, "Two men are standing over someone, Mr. Rush, I think. They're yelling at him. He's tied up, but I think we can free him if we rush them from the front door."

"Let's go!" Mark whispered back.

CHAPTER 4

THE RESCUE

They went quickly around to the partly open door and stopped just outside. Two stocky men stood inside and to their left, looming threateningly over the bound man on the floor. Just as one of the men kicked their help-less victim, Mark and David charged through the door.

The kidnappers spun around in shocked surprise. David and Mark had been trained in karate and now they used it with swift efficiency. As one of the men reached for a gun, David delivered a powerful thrust-ing kick to his midsection. Meanwhile Mark stopped the man before him with one blow to the neck. Both men went down at once.

"That'll keep them for a while! They're not serious-ly injured—just slowed down." Mark said grimly. He turned and knelt beside Mr. Rush, taking out his knife to cut a rope for the second time that day. "I hope this doesn't get to be a habit," he told David. He sliced away and quickly freed the engineer's mouth, hands, and feet.

"Are you all right, Mr. Rush?"

Rush couldn't answer at once. He groaned from the

pain in his leg where he'd been kicked.

"Help me get him up, David," Mark urged. The boys got the bruised man to his feet and helped him limp out the door. He leaned against the shed.

David ducked back into the cabin; he'd seen something he wanted the check.

"Who's your friend, Mark?" Rush gasped.

"That's David Curtis, sir," Mark said as he helped the trim black man stand erect. Rush straightened himself with difficulty, keeping one hand on Mark's shoulder as he got his balance back. David emerged from the cabin, and Rush looked at him. "Glad you're here, David!"

"Me too, Mr. Rush!" David replied. He'd found two pistols in belted holsters on the table in the cabin; keeping one, he gave the other to Mark. "Mark, there's a radio inside. Why don't I wreck it so those two can't call their buddies when they come to?"

"Great idea! Tear it up!" Mark turned to the older man. "Mr. Rush, let's get you out of here. Can you walk?"

"I *will* walk, Mark!" he answered. "Those men had just opened my briefcase and found that I'd tricked them. The report they wanted isn't there. They knocked me out of the chair. You two came just in time. Can you get that briefcase for me?"

"Yes, sir," Mark replied. He dashed in the cabin, retrieved the briefcase from the table, and brought it out.

David, meanwhile, was smashing the radio with the

butt of the unloaded pistol. "They won't use this again!" he said.

With one last glance at the kidnappers, he ran outside, slamming the door behind him.

Suddenly they heard a car's motor in the distance.

"That's headed this way, Mark!" David said. "Let's get out of here!"

The three turned quickly toward the kidnapper's parked car and the hill behind. As they began to climb, David stopped. "I want a look in that car," he said excitedly as he dashed over to the sedan.

He peered in—the keys were in the ignition! "Go ahead, Mark. I think I can drive this car down the trail and block it." He yanked open the door, slid behind the wheel, and started the engine.

"Just hurry," Mark called as he let Rush lean on him. "They're close, Mr. Rush! Can you climb this hill with us? We've got a plane on the other side."

"I think I can, Mark. But if I can't keep up, you two go ahead. Don't let me slow you down."

"We're not leaving without you!" Mark insisted.

They moved more quickly now, scrambling around trees and thick bushes, climbing the steep grade. Mark still held one of Mr. Rush's arms, but the engineer was gaining strength as he used his injured leg.

Meanwhile, David had backed the car around, slammed on the brakes, pointed it downhill, and driven carefully to the top of the narrow tracks in front of the cabin. Once there, he noticed a gully running down each side of the rough trail; this gave him another idea. He drove the car to the right until both wheels on that side were in the gully. Once it started, the car would head straight down. With its wheels locked in the gully, it couldn't turn. And the road was too narrow for another vehicle to pass!

David put the gears in neutral, took his foot off the brake, jumped out, and gave the vehicle a strong shove. The sedan began to roll, picking up speed. The gully kept it on a straight course down the hill as it gained momentum.

The noise of the approaching car was very loud now. David knew he should run, but he had to see what happened! Running back a few yards, he crouched behind a clump of bushes and watched the plummeting black car as it bounced downhill, faster and faster with each yard.

Just then a gray Land Rover careened around a curve in the trail fifty yards below, thick red dust swirling in the air behind.

Instantly the driver of the Land Rover spotted the black vehicle plunging toward him. He stood on the brakes and pounded the horn! The brakes locked, and the Land Rover rocked from side to side as it skidded upwards. Then it shuddered to a violent stop in a cloud of choking dust, directly before the bouncing black car.

David watched, mesmerized, as doors flew open on both sides of the Land Rover and men bolted frantically into the bush.

The car hit the rocking Land Rover with a metal-tearing crash, skidded along its left side and sheared off the spare gas tank. The sedan burst into flame. David heard men yelling as they tried to fight their way through the thick brush, but their voices were suddenly drowned in the explosion of the Land Rover's shattered side tank. Flames shot up and thick oily smoke rushed into the sky. Another tank exploded.

Suddenly David came to a sense of his own danger! With his ears ringing from the violent explosions and his eyes stunned by the brilliant flames, he turned from the bushes and raced uphill after Mark and Mr. Rush. The men behind him were armed and they were mad. With their prisoner and two vehicles gone, they'd be desperate! It was time to get out.

He ran a short way, then slowed to a fast walk. The incline was just too steep to run! By the time he reached the top his heart was pounding and he was gasping for breath. He paused and looked back. Trees hid the cabin and the road, but smoke from the burning cars towered above the forest, making a black smirch against a beautiful clear blue sky. David turned and headed downhill.

He was skidding on loose soil and gravel when he reached the bottom and raced for the plane. Mark and Mr. Rush were already strapped in and waiting anxiously for him.

"There he is!" Mark whooped with joy as he saw his friend dashing toward the plane. He started the engine as David ran for the open door and threw himself in the seat beside him. Rush, in the back seat, leaned forward and pounded David's shoulder.

As David fumbled for his own seat belt, Mark bounced the plane over the rough ground to the road, checking instruments as they moved. He turned onto the road and the Cessna picked up speed. But the road was rough—it took all Mark's skill to keep the craft straight along the bumpy surface. Finally, the plane lifted off! They were in the air!

The Cessna soared upward turning toward home. Behind them, the thick column of smoke from the burning vehicles poured into the sky, visible for miles around.

CHAPTER 5

THE FAMILY

"**W**ait a minute!" Mr. Daring said, laughing at Mark and David. "Let me catch my breath!" It was half past five and Mark, David and Tom Rush had just landed. Mark had radioed his dad as soon as they'd taken off and told him they were returning "with the bacon." Daring had known at once that meant Tom Rush. When they arrived, he took them to his office for the whole story.

Daring shook his head in wonder. "So you put the kidnappers out of action, tore out their radio, left them senseless on the floor, escaped with Tom, and blew up their two cars? Is that all you two have done since I told you to be careful?"

"Actually, Dad, it was one car and one Land Rover," Mark corrected.

"What a day's work!" his father said wonderingly. "I don't like the fact you've been in such great danger, but you did do what I asked—bring Tom Rush back. That's all I can say! What do you think, Tom?"

"I'll never forget the sight of them charging into that shed and wiping out those crooks. Talk about achieving tactical surprise! And blowing up those cars!

The marines would've been proud!" He had recovered from the rough treatment he'd received and was anxious to have the kidnappers put away.

"Did you call the police, Mr. Daring?" David asked.

"I called the army," he replied. "Colonel Lamumba is a friend. He's in charge of this district, and we've worked together on business we're doing for the government. I called right after Ed radioed that you were following Rush. The colonel said he'd get some men there right away."

Daring turned his head suddenly. Motioning the others to silence, he rose and stepped quietly toward the door. Carefully he turned the knob—then yanked the door wide open.

John Erickson, one of his engineers, stood before him, his mouth open in sudden surprise. Erickson was clearly caught off guard. He recovered quickly.

"I was just bringing this report, Jim," he said. "You asked for it this morning." His eyes searched the room swiftly and lingered on Tom Rush. "Hi, Tom, glad you're back safe."

"Thanks, John," Tom replied with genuine feeling. "So am I."

Erickson turned to Mr. Daring. "Jim, would you tell me what's happened?"

"Sure, John. Let me finish with the boys. Then I'll come by your office," Daring answered.

"Well, uh . . . sure," Erickson replied. He hesitated, shuffled awkwardly, and said, "See you later, then."

Turning quickly, he left the room. David was sure the man was disappointed.

Daring closed the door; he and Tom Rush looked soberly at each other. It seemed no one wanted to speak. Finally Tom said, "How long was he there, Jim, and how much did he hear?"

Daring frowned. "I don't know. I thought I heard someone at the door just after we came in, but I wasn't sure. He might have been there the whole time. Something's not right here."

Mark and David looked at each other, but kept their mouths shut. The older men were trusting them with a very serious information, just by letting them stay in the room. Obviously they'd discussed Erickson before.

Daring sat down. "I think we'll let it go for now. Colonel Lamumba told me he'd sent an army helicopter to the cabin. Just before you got back, he called to say that the soldiers had found four men there. Two of them were the ones you surprised; the others had some broken bones and burns. The soldiers are bringing them all to the colonel's headquarters. If you and Tom can identify them as kidnappers, they'll be jailed."

He paused. "Two of the men are definitely connected with Hoffmann and Walther—the ones we saw at the airport. They're bad news and we think they're part of a scan to steal mining rights. They might kill prospectors, steal their claim papers and file claims for the land themselves. The good news is that the colonel says we're closing in on them now."

This news cheered them all! Daring added, "The colonel is very pleased to have captured these men." He paused and rubbed his chin. "The others got away—they were on foot—and must have melted into the hills before the soldiers arrived. But I don't think-they will be troubling anyone for a while, not without transportation, and especially not now that they know the army is alerted." He beamed at the boys with unbounded pride and pleasure.

"Good!" Mark said, and David agreed. "When do we go?"

"Tomorrow morning. You can all fly to the army headquarters after breakfast and be back by mid-morning." Daring thought a moment. "Perhaps we'd better not tell the rest of the family about this until Colonel Lamumba gives the word."

Daring turned to Rush. "Well, Tom, you've had a busy day. I'll go tell John a little of what happened. Make two copies of your report, put them in the safe, and give me the original." He started to leave, then turned back. "How about bringing Phyllis and the kids over for a swim before supper? The water will be good for your sore muscles!"

"Thanks, Jim. That might help." Rush stood up slowly, obviously still sore, straightened, grinned at the boys, and left the room.

"Dad, Mr. Rush sure has stamina!" Mark observed admiringly. "Those men tied him up and kicked him around. Then he scrambled up and down a steep hill to get to the plane."

Daring looked at his son with a curious expression. "Don't you know what he did before he joined us?" Mark shook his head.

"He was a Marine infantry officer. It'll take a lot more than that to put him down." Daring chuckled. "Remind me to tell you about him sometime." From his manner the boys could see that they had a lot to learn about the quiet black engineer Mr. Daring trusted so much. Daring stood up. "But let's go home now. And remember, keep the details to yourselves till I get the word from Colonel Lamumba."

In a short while the pool was packed with the two families and half a dozen extra kids. Mark and David let their frayed nerves unwind as they played with the younger ones in the water. By the time they'd showered and sat down to supper, however, the day's exertions began to catch up with them.

"You boys are silent as tombstones," Penny teased. "Did we wear you out playing water polo? I thought you were both in great shape?"

Little Ruth chimed in, "And I caught up with David when he tried to get away. He's not so fast!" she laughed.

David tickled her neck before she could stop his hand. "You're too quick for me, Ruthie."

"We sort of wore ourselves out climbing hills while we waited for Mr. Rush," Mark said. "I think I'll turn in now, Mom." He pushed back from the table.

They said goodnight to Penny and headed straight to bed. After they'd read their Bibles for a few minutes—a habit they'd both trained themselves to do—Mark reached for the lamp and looked at David. "Ready for me to turn out the light?"

"You bet I am," David said, closing his Bible and stretching out. "What a day!"

Mark switched off the light. Except for a shaft of moonlight that peeped in from the window, the room was completely dark.

It was David's custom to review the events of the day before he went to sleep. It had all happened so fast! Would he be able to recognize those men who had bolted from the Land Rover just before it exploded? He tried it now, but all in a few minutes he was asleep.

CHAPTER 6

"THE OTHERS GOT AWAY!"

The white-trimmed green Cessna lifted off smoothly, climbed into a completely cloudless sky, and then turned eastward. "We'll be there in half an hour," Mark said to David, who sat beside him. Tom Rush was in back, reading engineering reports.

David studied both the land and the map, trying to familiarize himself with the country over which they were flying. Mark's dad had told David that he would check him out in the Cessna so he could share the flying with Mark, and David wanted to learn all he could so he'd be ready.

They flew over grasslands and crossed a wide, dark river that wound from north to south before they saw the army district headquarters. Mark radioed the tower, received permission to land, and brought the plane down onto a wide runway.

"This beats landing on that rough road by a long shot!" Mark said, slowing the plane for the turn.

"It sure does," David agreed, remembering the harrowing experience of the day before.

Mark taxied back toward the headquarters building, passing camouflage-painted helicopters and fighter planes parked beside the runway. A jeep drove toward them, and the driver waved for them to follow. Mark taxied behind the vehicle until they came to a parking place beside the last military aircraft and just in front of the two-story concrete headquarters building.

Climbing out of the plane, they all felt the oppressive heat of the low land by the river. A burly sergeant in green fatigues got out of the jeep and asked them to follow him to Colonel Lamumba's office. The three men followed him into the building, down a hall to their left, and into a large office. Soldiers were working in the outer office, and one of these picked up a phone and informed the colonel that they had arrived. Then he rose from his desk and led them into the colonel's office.

David looked around the office. It looked more like a hunting lodge! Long, curved, hunting bows hung from racks on one wall. Several very long fighting spears with iron tips and brightly painted shields decorated another. A magnificent set of horns framed a large photograph of lions. Three males were crouched in the foreground staring with great menace at the camera. David wondered what had happened after the picture was taken! And if the photographer had survived!

Colonel Lamumba stood up when they were announced and came around the desk to greet them. A large man, his well-muscled frame filled out a tailored khaki uniform to perfection.

"Mr. Rush, it's good to see you again! I can't wait to discuss our find in the hills. And Mark, it's been too long since you've visited here. How are you?" He shook their hands warmly.

"So this is the young man who demolishes enemy vehicles!" he said with a broad smile, shaking David's hand.

David was surprised and at the same time curious. Obviously Mr. Daring had told him about their adventures the day before! The colonel was clearly pleased at what David had done. But what was "the find in the hills?" What was going on here?

"Sit down, gentlemen," he said in a deep voice, waving to chairs. He waited for them to sit, then pulled up a chair.

He and Rush immediately began talking about the project Daring's mining firm was doing for the government. David realized from their talk that the army was somehow involved.

Within a few minutes the colonel called a corporal into the office to record their conversation, and began to question Tom Rush and the boys about the events of the previous day. As they talked, the colonel kept glancing at the notes which Rush had given him, asking questions occasionally. This took over half an hour.

Colonel Lamumba rose. "Well, let's go identify these men," he said. He led them out of the room, down the hall, outside under the hot sun, and into another building. Here they waited in a room with a large one-way glass window set in an interior wall. They could see the people inside, but the people could not see them. In a few minutes soldiers brought four men into the room behind the glass.

"Do you recognize any of them?" the colonel asked.

"I sure do!" Rush said. He pointed out the two stocky men who had kidnapped him. The boys also identified them as the men they had surprised in the cabin.

"Excellent," Lamumba said, beaming at the two boys with grim satisfaction. "You did a great job putting them out of action, gentlemen. We are charging them with armed robbery and kidnapping. They will be kept here as their case is processed. You would not believe the violence we're having to deal with in connection with our nation's diamond mines. Tell your father, Mark, that we are grateful for your help in getting these men."

"What about the other two?" he asked. "Can you identify them?"

None of the three—Rush, Mark, or David—had seen them before. One had his arm in a sling and a bandage on his head. The shirt of the other was bulging around thick bandages beneath. Both had cuts on their arms and faces.

The colonel explained, "These men were hurt getting away from the burning cars. One broke an arm; the other broke several ribs. They are willing to testify against their employers in order to get a lighter sentence." The big soldier looked gravely at Mark and David. Then his teeth flashed white against his dark skin as he smiled and then he confirmed what they already suspected. "Your father, Mark, told me all about your raid on the cabin. Perhaps you gentlemen would like to enlist in our army? My officers and I like the way you approach tactical problems!"

"Thank you, sir," Mark replied. Lamumba then led them out of the room and back toward the other building. He invited them to stay for lunch, but they declined with thanks. "We've got to get back," Rush said.

"I understand," Colonel Lamumba replied. "In that case, you leave with my gratitude. We are searching for the other men who were in that Land Rover. As soon as we capture them, I will let you know."

He shook hands and bade them farewell at the door of his office building. Just as they began to walk away, he called to Mark, "I almost forgot! Please tell your father that I have been studying the game of chess and that if he uses that queen's pawn opening again, I will have a great surprise for him."

"Yes, sir," Mark answered. "Dad wiped me out with that opening last week. I know it's not invincible, but it sure beats me! I'll give him your warning." The colonel laughed and waved good-bye.

They flew home and after reporting to Mr. Daring went to the room where Mark worked and examined the mining reports he'd been assigned. The more David studied them, the more he realized the extent of

Mr. Daring's diamond mining operation.

"Time for lunch, boys," Mr. Daring announced, entering the office. "If anyone asks about your visit to the colonel today, be brief in your answers. The less said, the less likely others will learn what we know about the colonel's plans to capture the rest of the gang."

"Has the colonel captured most of the gang, Dad?" Mark asked as he closed his file and stretched.

"We don't know," his father replied. "They've got four of them. But Hoffmann and Walther are still at large and we think they're the big guys in the gang. We don't know how many others are with them. It's not over yet."

They left the office building and walked toward the house. "David, you said that at least four men jumped out of the Land Rover before it caught fire," Daring continued. "Two got hurt from falls in the brush and were captured. But the other two got away. They had no car, so they had to go across country on foot. So far, they seem to have vanished, and we don't know where."

They dropped the subject as they came to the house. There they washed for lunch, and joined the family in the dining room. A friend of Penny's was there, a friendly dark-haired girl named Jeanne, whose father worked at the agricultural station down the road. She was also a friend of Mark's, or so it seemed from the way they teased each other during the meal.

"Jeanne works with Mom and me in our home

school," Penny told David. "Several families pitch in on this. We teach the younger kids."

"I hope you enjoy your visit, David," Jeanne said. "How long will you be here?" she asked.

"Two months—if Mrs. Daring is willing to feed me that long," he answered. "Penny, would you please pass the sandwiches?"

They all laughed as Penny passed the plate across the table. David took a sandwich, then handed it quickly back to Penny just as Mark reached for the plate.

"Hey!" Mark said. "I'll take one too!"

"I thought you were on a diet, Mark," his sister said seriously, holding the plate.

"You'll know I'm on a diet when I tell you, Sis. Hand me those sandwiches." She laughed and passed them over, glancing at David. He grinned.

That afternoon, Mr. Daring took David up in the Cessna for a final check. Then he let David take the pilot's seat while he rode as passenger. David flew around and made several landings and takeoffs. Daring recognized at once that David was fully competent to handle the aircraft.

As they came in for the last landing, the older man told him, "Actually, David, your dad is the one who persuaded me to let Mark learn to fly. It was a good idea. It's been a great help to me and the firm and a lot of fun for Mark."

Daring went back to his office and David joined Mark once again. The boys spent the rest of the afternoon on Mark's projects, which David found increasingly interesting. At the end of the day they joined the family at the pool. The sun was close to the horizon and the bright orange colors were brilliant in the late afternoon sky. The air was still warm enough to make the water of the pool feel refreshing and invigorating.

After supper Mark, Penny, and David took a walk, strolling under the tall trees that framed the drive to their home. They sauntered down the road, past the offices and labs. The sounds of Africa—its birds, insects, animals—were all around them. A half-moon lit the area with a golden haze, and they walked in and out of the shadows cast by the dark trees. The heavy sweet smell of wildflowers surrounded them as they strolled. To David it seemed like an enchanted evening.

"How do you like Africa, David?" Penny asked as she walked between the two boys. "You haven't gotten bored visiting us, have you?"

"Bored? Not on your life!" he replied with fervor, glancing over her head at Mark. "Life here really goes a little faster than I'm used to." He laughed. "I've only been here three days but it seems like a lot has happened!"

Mark gave him a warning shake of his head, reminding him not to reveal anything. But David was careful. "Mark and I have flown all over the place these last two days!"

"When will we go up-country and take the canoe

trip, Mark?" she asked.

"I thought we'd do that Monday. Can you get free then?"

"Yes. Mom told me just to let her know two days ahead of time, so she could plan the children's school-work without me. And Dad said I could go anytime next week. I'm ahead of schedule with the work I'm doing for him." She sounded excited at the prospect of the trip.

"Fine," Mark answered. "Let's plan on it."

"David, these canoe trips are so much fun," Penny said. "As I said before, we fly up-country in the morning, and paddle a canoe downriver for about six hours. I photograph all kinds of birds and flowers. Then Dad picks us up and we fly back. It's like being in another world! We do the whole thing in a day. There's a boat that takes the canoe back upstream for us."

"Great!" David said. He was glad to learn that Penny would go with them. He was liking Africa more each day.

CHAPTER 7

TO THE CITY

The aroma of the muffins crept from the kitchen, snaked its way down the hall, and surrounded David as he was reading his Bible. He had showered after his morning run with Mark and Mr. Daring, and was deep in the book of Nehemiah getting ready for the family Bible study time when the muffin attack tested his discipline. He wrestled manfully with this temptation for a few minutes before he decided he really ought to help Mrs. Daring in the kitchen. After all, he'd promised his mom that he would. What better time than now?

Strolling casually into the spacious kitchen, he found her humming a cheerful tune as she prepared breakfast. "Hi! Can I help?"

"You certainly can, David," her blue eyes sparkled with habitual good humor. She had a peaceful nature just like Penny's. "Start by testing this muffin for me—the butter's on the table." She held out a full plate, and David took a hot muffin and began spreading butter on it.

"Did you sleep well?" she asked as she got out the plates.

"Yes, ma'am, I sure did," he said around bites.

"We're getting great exercise, and we've been so busy that when I go to bed I conk out right away. That sure was a good muffin." He licked his fingers.

"You'd better have another one, then," and she held out the plate again. "You know, David, we're so glad you could come. Jim and I have loved staying in touch with your family all these years, and our children are delighted to have you here. They have some fine friends in this country, but you mean so much to them. When Penny was little, she used to ask if you couldn't be her brother like Mark was. And Mark asked the same thing."

She smiled affectionately at him. Then a buzzer went off, and she turned to open the oven. "How about putting the plates on the table?" she asked.

David took the plates into the dining room and returned to the kitchen as she began to stir the eggs.

"Anything else?" he asked.

"Not yet," she answered. "Make yourself comfortable."

Light from the early morning sun streamed in through the wide windows, and David could see the mountains in the distance, almost blue with haze. Mark had told him that they would hike in those mountains on this visit. What adventures awaited them there?

"When will Mom and Dad get my letters?" he asked. He'd written from London, and also when he'd arrived at the Darings.

"Eight days, David," she replied. "Just eight days. They'll be so glad to hear from you. And don't forget, we'll call them by shortwave radio this weekend. That's always fun." She got out glasses and began pouring the fruit juice.

Then Penny came in, smiling and bright. "Sorry I'm late, Mom," she said. She hurried to put knives and forks on the table, flashing David a smile as she passed. His mouth was full of muffin, so he could only wave back.

"How about a muffin, David," she asked innocently. He looked so embarrassed that she burst out laughing. "Oh, I see! You've already had one! Or two! Goodness, how many have you eaten?"

"Leave that man alone, Penny, or he'll get his feelings hurt and go on a hunger strike," her mother warned.

Finally David finished his mouthful and was able to reply. "Yeah, Penny, your mom's right! If you're not careful, I'm liable to go on a strike—after breakfast." This girl flustered him sometimes; it was a funny feeling and he didn't quite understand it.

"It'll be *after* breakfast, all right," she laughed. She quickly set out the glasses.

Then the rest of the family came in and they all sat down. Mr. Daring led the prayer, as always, and soon they were enjoying eggs, muffins, bananas, and grapefruit.

Mr. Daring finished first, and then he began the morning's Bible study by reading from the second chapter of Nehemiah. He reminded the family of Nehemiah's prayer in the previous chapter and of his complete dependence on God's love and commitment to His people. For several minutes they talked about Nehemiah's approach to the king.

"Look how Nehemiah did his homework," he said, "and how he was ready to give an answer when the king asked what help he needed. He was ready for whatever was to come." After that Mr. Daring led them in prayer. Then it was time for them all to get to their work. Ruth and Benjamin had schooling with Penny this morning.

Mark and David walked down the drive with Mr. Daring to the office. On the way he broke the news. "Boys, Colonel Lamumba sent a message by helicopter yesterday afternoon. The men they captured have really talked! He's learned a lot about the gang that's moving in on the mining companies, especially on the exploration teams. They intend to steal as many mines as possible. He warned me to tell our people to be very alert. Hoffmann and Walther—those men I pointed out at the airport—are in the middle of all this trouble, but there isn't enough evidence yet to pull them in." He fell silent as they walked under the tall trees in the cool morning breeze.

"I don't want the family to be alarmed about any of this," Mr. Daring continued, "so keep it to yourselves. But I want you two to keep your eyes open. I'll need your help." He paused a minute, and the boys sensed he was going to tell them more than he'd revealed so far.

"We've just discovered an area rich in diamonds. Our research—Tom Rush was in charge of that— proves that we've made a major find in the Larumba Valley."

He stopped before they got to the office building. "We need to file proper papers. We have help from within the government, and we're confident we can get this done properly—and in time."

The boys glanced at each other as they followed Mr. Daring into his office. Inside, he shut the door and waved them to the chairs flanking his desk.

Then Mr. Daring dropped his bombshell. "I'd like you two to take a report to our lawyer in Nairobi. When he gets it he can file the paperwork. Our firm will then have the legal rights we need to pursue the development of the new mine. He sat back in his chair.

"When do you want us to go, Dad?" Mark saw the possibility of more excitement for the two of them, and his face lit up with a smile.

"When do you go?" Daring repeated the question. "Ten o'clock this morning. That gives you some time to work here for a while. I'll come back and go to the house with you to get your packs."

Mark and David jumped up and headed for the door.

"By the way, Mark," he added, "when you get to the city, take the car; it'll be in the hangar. You know where Johnston's law office is; just get our papers to him. Then you can show David some of the sights in that area before flying home." The boys turned back toward the door, and he added casually, "Penny might like to go too, if you ask her."

"Great!" David said; then his face reddened. Mr. Daring had been talking to Mark, not him! But they pretended not to notice.

"Fine, Dad," Mark replied, "I'll ask her."

The boys worked on the field reports and maps for the next two hours, Mark continuing to explain them to David. David was feeling more and more at home in this work. They were so engrossed in their studies that they didn't notice the time. They were completely surprised when Mark's dad come in the office and announced, "Let's go get your packs."

Mark had already called and talked with Penny, so she was ready by the time they came. As Mark and David stuffed their packs with the emergency gear and supplies that they always carried with them, she joined them.

She had her pack in her hand. "I'm ready," she announced excitedly. "Thanks for including me."

"Oh, I guess we can stand it," Mark replied casually, "if you don't chatter, that is. What do you think, David?"

"As long as she doesn't talk, Mark; she's got to keep quiet."

"You guys are crazy," she laughed.

Mr. Daring drove them to the plane. On the way, Penny began to tell David about the canoe trip she and

Mark had planned. "That will be the highlight of your visit!" she said brightly. "We take a whole day to drift down the river. It's terrific for taking pictures." Like her mother, she was a photographer and planned to take many shots of the birds and flowers on the river with her telephoto lens.

"We also watch for pythons and wild pigs—and especially for crocodiles," Mark added.

"We do not!" she replied. "Those crocodiles are in another part of the river. We don't even go close to them!"

"Where do you keep the canoe?" David asked.

"At the medical mission," she replied. "Dr. Hawkins runs the clinic and he lets us use his boat. There's so much to see on the river. It's just fascinating!"

Soon they were in the air, headed for the city. But David began to wonder about the crocodiles.

CHAPTER 8

THE AMBUSH

They left the Cessna in care of the company's mechanic and got in the station wagon. Mark drove, taking the airport road toward the city several miles away. This road was rather narrow, winding through woods with very tall trees on both sides. Bright red, yellow, and white flowers decorated the heavy green underbrush.

Mark was as careful a driver as he was a pilot, David noted. Penny sat between the boys, their packs in the back seat. None of them noticed the green sedan that pulled out from a hangar at the airport and followed them, staying behind at some distance.

Five minutes from the airport, however, Penny turned to get something out of her pack and saw the car through the back window as it came around a curve. Instantly the sedan slowed down, but it didn't turn off the road. It just stayed far behind. *That's odd*, she thought to herself. She began to look back whenever they went around curves—and the same thing happened! The sedan slowed quickly as it came into sight, but kept following.

"Mark, there's a car behind us and its acting kind of strange."

"I've been watching it," Mark replied.

David turned and looked past her through the back window. "What's strange about it, Penny?" he asked.

"It slows down just as it comes around a turn, almost as if the driver doesn't want us to see him. It's done that twice. Maybe I'm silly, Mark, but it gives me a strange feeling." She wondered if she were being foolish, but Mark took her seriously.

"You're not being silly, Penny," Mark said at once. "Dad wants us to keep our eyes open on this trip." He looked quickly at David. Both boys wondered if this were what Mr. Daring had warned them about.

"Let's not take any chances, Mark," David said. "What we've got with us is important." He looked serious, and Penny wondered what he was talking about. But she was relieved that they took her own fears seriously.

"Right," Mark agreed. "Dad didn't think anything funny would happen at this end though, or he sure wouldn't have let Penny come along. I'll speed up. Let's see if that car does too."

He gradually increased speed, and then held it steady. He was glad that there was no traffic on this part of the road because they were really moving! He tried to recall what was ahead—some woods, he remembered, and a swamp as well before they got to the fields. Then came the suburbs. He was very alert. They had to get the report to the lawyer's office, and they had to keep Penny safe.

David was watching the car through the side mirror. Keeping his voice calm, he said, "He seems to have picked up speed, Mark. Are there side roads we could take if we wanted to shake him?"

"Not for several miles," Mark replied. "Not till we pass the swamp. Then we come to some roads and houses. Johnston's office is in the suburbs, not downtown, so we don't have very far to go."

"He's getting closer," David said quickly. "Can you keep him from passing? If he wants the report we're taking to Johnston, he might try to force us off the road!"

"You bet I can!" Mark replied grimly. "I'll stay in the middle of the road. He'll never get by."

But just then the road curved sharply, and as they came around the turn they saw a Land Rover directly ahead of them, parked across the road. Men were standing on either side. It was a roadblock!

"Mark!" Penny cried—but her brother had already seen it. David had been looking back; he whipped his head around and was shocked to see the Land Rover looming before them. Mark would have to jam the brakes to keep from crashing into the other vehicle.

Mark yelled, "Hold tight!" and hit the brakes. The car skidded and slowed. David's right hand shot up and grabbed the handle above the door while he threw his left arm around Penny and held her close as the car swerved. The nose of the station wagon lifted as Mark released the brakes, turned left and hit the gas. The vehicle bounced across the rough edge of the road, rammed through the brush, and staggered back onto the pavement. Mark stepped on the gas and the vehicle leaped ahead.

Two men dove into the bush to avoid being run over. A blond-haired man leaped back from the road. "Is that Hoffmann?" David asked.

"I couldn't see," Penny replied as the station wagon increased speed.

Looking in the side mirror, David saw men scrambling out of the bushes. The green car had skidded to a stop—the driver was not about to do what Mark had done. Then the road curved again and they were out of sight.

"Great job, Mark!" David said. "Great job! We've got a good head start." He still held Penny.

"Oh, Mark, that was wonderful driving," she said. Her heart was pounding.

"Thank the Lord," Mark answered gratefully. "I sure didn't want to stop and let them capture us."

The road swerved again; now they were racing past the swamp. Suddenly a crossroad appeared, then some houses, and then another road. Mark kept going, but around the next curve he slowed quickly and turned sharply right. The vehicle swayed around the turn and settled on the new path. Then, at the corner, Mark turned left and gradually decreased speed as he passed two blocks of homes. He turned right again. David and Penny were confused, but Mark knew exactly where he was going.

"This is an expensive neighborhood," he said, "with lots of government people and foreign businessmen living in it. We'll be at Johnston's in a minute." He turned left once more, and they passed small office buildings. Suddenly he pulled in between two of these and parked the station wagon behind the far one.

"Take the package, David, while I lock the car."

David grabbed the package with the mining application, and he and Penny ran up half a dozen steps into the building. Mark joined them at once and led them quickly down a hall to Johnston's office.

A secretary was seated at the desk facing the door. When Mark had identified himself, she led them at once into Mr. Johnston's office. "He's expecting you," she said and then closed the door behind them.

Mr. Johnston greeted them warmly. "Welcome, Mark and Penny." He shook their hands. "This must be David," he said and shook David's hand as well.

This tall, tanned Englishman handled legal affairs for many of the foreign businesses in the country. He waved them to plush chairs and then sat down himself. "I've been expecting you." His lean face was topped by jet black hair and his blue eyes peered out from horn-rimmed glasses.

Quickly Mark told him what had happened. As he finished, he said, "I'd like to call Dad right away, sir, to let him know that people were waiting for us. They must have a spy in our office." The frown on his face showed his concern

"Call from here, Mark," Johnston said. "At least you got the papers to me. We'll make copies right away, store them in our safe, and get the originals to the proper agency. I can get police protection for us before we leave the office. I'll use the secretary's phone. You use mine to call your father." He left the room while Mark called his dad.

Mr. Daring answered at once, and Mark quickly described the attempted ambush. "They knew we were coming, Dad," he concluded.

David stood and walked over to the window while Mark talked. He searched the street, but saw no sign of the green sedan or the Land Rover that had chased them. He turned back as Mark hung up.

"Dad says to come back right away. He's sorry he put us in danger," Mark told them. "Of course he couldn't have known this would happen." He looked at his sister. "We can thank you for that, Penny. You spotted the car and warned us. I'm glad you came along!"

Penny's face flushed with pleasure at her brother's tribute. "It was your driving that got us around that Land Rover! They had us trapped."

Mr. Johnston came back into the office. He was smiling. "The police are sending a car right away to take me to the government office with your father's papers. You can follow us in your car. Then the police will go with you to the airport and make sure you're safe."

The three youngsters relaxed visibly. At least they'd

be safe with a police escort! Johnston chatted with them until his secretary came in and said the police had arrived.

The genial lawyer checked the copy his secretary had made of Daring's report, and then led them outside. "The police want you to show them where you were ambushed." He paused. "You don't know how important this is. You people have done a splendid job." He shook hands with each of them. "Good-bye! Take care!"

He got in the squad car with the two officers. Mark, Penny, and David got in the station wagon and followed him to a government office downtown. Then the police led them back to the airport road. Mark pulled off the road when they came to the place of the roadblock, and the police car parked behind them.

Here they all got out while the officers studied the road and the grass beside it, asking questions about the ambush. One of the policemen photographed the tire tracks. The underbrush was torn where Mark had gone off the road, but the pursuers and the vehicles had disappeared. The police then led them to the airport and waited while Mark, David, and the mechanic made a careful inspection of the plane.

"Did anyone come asking about us while we were gone?" Mark asked the mechanic as they went over the Cessna.

"No one," he replied. "We've kept a watch on the plane, but we've seen no one." Their flight plan was ready, so the three thanked the policemen and got in the Cessna.

Mark started the engine and prepared for takeoff. A strong breeze rocked the small plane as he taxied to the end of the runway. In a few minutes the tower cleared him for takeoff and soon they were in the air, gaining altitude.

"I was looking forward to shopping," Penny said sadly, speaking above the noise of the engine. "And we wanted to show you some of the sights, David. I'm so sorry all this had to happen."

"If you hadn't been so alert, we would have been in big trouble," David replied seriously. "But I'll hold you to that promise to show me the city, and Mark and I will buy you an expensive lunch for saving us from those hoodlums. Maybe two hamburgers!" He smiled at Penny.

She looked at him for a long moment, still troubled. Then her spirits lifted, and she smiled back. But she wondered where the men that had put up the roadblock had gone. Would they see them again? And where?

CHAPTER 9

ARE THE TROUBLES OVER?

Mr. Daring was deeply disturbed. He'd met them when they landed and had taken them directly to his office. Now he was sitting behind his desk, worry written all over his face, while Penny, Mark, and David sat across from him.

"I would never have sent you with that package if I'd thought for a minute that you'd be in danger."

"We know that, Dad," Mark replied. "But I don't think there was any real danger. They wanted the mining report we were carrying. They wouldn't want to bring the police and the army out for kidnapping us."

"Perhaps you're right, Mark," his father answered. He slumped in his chair, arms across his chest, eyes troubled.

David spoke up then. "What worries us, sir, is the fact that those men were waiting for us. They knew we were coming. And there's something else—we think they must have talked with each other by radio—the men in the sedan and Land Rover, I mean. Because the

68

green car was racing to catch up with us just as we came to the Land Rover blocking the road. They had it planned all the way."

Mr. Daring nodded soberly. "I think you're right, David." Then he looked at his son. "Mark, you must have done a great job of driving! I bet those guys were stunned!" He seemed to perk up at the thought. "You young people have outsmarted them at every turn."

"Penny put us on the alert," David added. "She noticed that the sedan was sticking close behind us."

"Mark was already watching them, though," Penny added.

"Boys, it took me a long time to realize that what people call 'woman's intuition' ought to be taken seriously. Carolyn has warned me of many things over the years, but I wouldn't pay any attention. Finally I learned." He looked from one to another. "Penny, I think you should stay with these two guys and keep them out of trouble."

"That's fine with me, Dad!" She smiled over at David—then blushed when she saw Mark's grin.

"Your mother will kill me for letting you kids get in danger," Daring said. "Let me explain the whole thing to her."

"Sure, Dad," Penny answered. She thought a moment. "Do you think she'll want to keep us all under lock and key from now on?" she asked. "That is, until they catch those men?" They had made so many plans for David's visit and suddenly Penny feared that their fun might be canceled.

Her dad laughed. "I hope not, Penny. I'll try to spring you loose from time to time. Let's go home and I'll tell her what happened." They followed him out of the office.

As they left the building, Mark let Penny and David walk ahead while he took his dad aside and asked quietly, "Do you know who called to tell those men we were coming, Dad?"

"Yes, Mark, I do. It was John Erickson." He walked thoughtfully beside his son for a few steps. Mark knew he was choosing his words with care.

"Erickson heard your call to me. He must have had a line on my phone. Boy, was I dumb to let him tap my own phone! When I finished talking to you, Rush came in and told me he'd tapped Erickson's line, and had just played back a call to those men who tried to stop you. That proves Erickson's a part of the gang that's stealing mining rights in Kenya. He's been a spy all along. I called the colonel at once. He said to grab Erickson and keep him until the army could send some soldiers for him."

"So did you get him?" Mark asked eagerly.

His father shook his head. "No. When I got to his office he had already gone. I ran outside, but he was just driving off. I called the colonel and told him which way Erickson was heading. Let's hope they pick him up."

Daring continued, "There's no telling what information he stole from us! But you kids sure beat him today, Mark! By getting that package to Johnston, you took the information those thieves wanted. They failed to steal our mine—and they're in big trouble."

Mark and his dad heard Penny and David laughing as they went up the steps to the house. The father and son grinned at each other. "Do you think those two are getting along O.K.?" Daring asked his son with a half-serious expression.

"I hope so, Dad," Mark replied, with equal gravity. Then they both laughed out loud, and followed Penny and David into the house. Once inside, they gathered in the living room and told the whole story to Mrs. Daring. She wasn't too happy about the danger the three teenagers had been in, but she knew they were capable young people.

"But John Erickson!" she exclaimed. "How could he betray you after all you've done for him, Jim? Why do you think he would do such a thing?"

"I don't know, honey," he replied. "I guess they offered him a lot of money to get the information they wanted. And we've both known for years that John has a real problem with coveting things he doesn't have. He's gotten himself in debt for years, buying things he can't afford. If people won't control their desires, they can end up in terrible trouble. I'm afraid that's what's happened to John."

"This diamond mine is a big find, Carolyn," he continued, "a real big find. You know what that means for us." He put his arm around her as they sat on the sofa.

Then he nodded briefly to Mark.

Mark took the signal. His mom and dad needed some time alone to talk. "I'm starving," he said, rising from the chair. "Let's get something to eat."

David and Penny followed him to the kitchen. With all that had happened they hadn't had lunch, so they rummaged around and put a platter of sandwiches together. When they'd finished, Penny went to the refrigerator and brought out some cold apple pie.

Finally satisfied, David pushed his chair back and looked over at Mark. "So, when do we get to explore those mountains you've told me about, Mark?"

"Not until we take the canoe trip, Mark!" Penny interrupted quickly. "You said we'd do that next."

"You're right," he answered. "First the canoe trip and then we'll get to the mountains." He paused, then added, "That is, if the folks will let us. After all that's happened . . . ." His voice trailed off.

"Oh, everything will calm down," Penny replied. "Those crooks won't dare show themselves now that the army's looking for them. I'm sure Mom and Dad will let us go."

The phone rang. Penny picked it up, listened for a moment, and said, "I'll call him." She looked over at Mark and David. "It's for Dad. I think it's Colonel Lamumba." She went to get her father.

Returning in a moment, she hung up the phone. "Dad went to the other phone. And he seems happy about whatever the colonel is telling him. I'm *sure* he'll let us take the canoe trip." She smiled.

Mr. Daring came in shortly afterwards, looking very pleased. "They picked up that gang in the sedan," he said. "The Land Rover escaped—it's probably hiding in a garage somewhere, but they caught the others. They're all linked with the troubles at the mining stations. What a coup!"

He looked at the three young people with obvious pride. "The colonel wants to make you all honorary lieutenants in his army's Special Forces; or he would if he could. In any case, he says to thank you again." Mr. Daring looked relieved. "Maybe our troubles are over now and we can settle down to some peace. Those guys won't be bothering us any more!"

Penny was as happy as the boys at the colonel's compliments. But she had a sudden feeling that their troubles were far from over. She shuddered slightly.

CHAPTER 10

THE VULTURES DESCEND

The great vultures spiraled menacingly above the narrow valley, waiting for the hyenas below to finish gorging on the carcass of the beast they had killed. In the valley itself the air was motionless, stifling, and oppressive as if invisible walls went up from the hills and blocked out the breeze. A narrow trace of a road disappeared under the trees at the upper end.

Inside the weathered cabin, the heat was intensified. Rifles leaned against one wall, while knapsacks littered the floor beside the weapons. Bunk beds stood against two of the dark walls, and the whole dingy place showed scars of abuse by the miners who had used it.

Sweat ran from the faces of the four angry men seated at the rough wooden table: two Africans, Mapunda and Kala, and the two Europeans, Walther and Hoffmann. Their tempers had risen to match the temperature of the sweltering air they breathed. Hoffmann and the two Africans were glaring at Walther.

"We have no choice, Walther." Hoffmann's eyes

74

glittered as he stared at his fellow countryman, the muscles of his neck bulging beneath an open khaki shirt. Thin blond hair topped a lean and angry face as he spoke again, his voice quiet with suppressed menace. "There's no other way."

Mapunda, at Hoffmann's right, was the largest man in the room, larger even than Walther. Triple lines of scars from tribal rituals covered both of his cheeks. So far, he had said nothing, but his stare never left Walther's sullen, red face.

Next to him sat Kala, the smallest—and most dangerous—man there. Everything about him appeared relaxed except his eyes. These had grown darker as his anger increased. Like Mapunda, he wore jungle fatigues. He held a pen in his small, elegant hand. His occasional gestures reminded them all of his renown as a knifefighter. His posture, as always, was nonchalant; inside, however, he was taut as a coiled snake. Kala spoke softly, the menace in his voice piercing the thick air they struggled to breathe.

"What else can we do, Walther? Half our team has been captured. Two of our vehicles are destroyed, another taken by the police. Erickson is gone. The only way we can get the mine now is to kidnap one of his children." He tapped the pen on the table to emphasize his point, holding it firmly but gently—as if it were a knife.

Walther grunted his disgust and stood up, his chair rasping across the rough wooden floor. As he reached his full height, rolled-back sleeves revealed powerful forearms. His skin never tanned, and his neck was as red as his angry face. Turning his back contemptuously on the others, he strode heavily to the open door and spoke without turning. "Four of our men are in Lamumba's jail, charged with kidnapping Tom Rush. They may never get out. Do you plan for us to join them?"

Hoffmann wanted to shout. They'd been over the whole thing for the past two hours. Struggling to control his rage, he glanced quickly at the two Africans and saw that they were still on his side. But he had to persuade Walther!

When he had gained control of himself, Hoffmann played his trump. "Schmidt did not send us here to fail, Walther. Do you not realize what will happen to you and me if we do?" Schmidt was the big boss, the brains behind this international gang of thieves, directing their actions from his office in Paris.

Walther's back stiffened. Hoffmann continued, "Schmidt wants that diamond mine. We must get the claim papers. We must force Daring to hand them over. And to do that . . ." Hoffmann paused, then spoke with quiet finality. "To do that, we must have something to trade. Something Daring loves more than a diamond mine. Something like his daughter."

He paused again. "It's as simple as that. And you and I, Walther . . ." His angry eyes bored into the sweat-stained khaki shirt stretched taut across Walther's broad back. "You and I have no other choice."

Hoffmann leaned back in his chair; he was finished. This was his last chance. He had messed up the plan too many times already. Hoffmann's hand dropped to the holstered pistol at his belt.

High above the valley the soaring vultures circled patiently, closer now, waiting for the remaining hyenas to leave. Two had already wandered off, stuffed; two remained. Standing in the doorway, Walther watched them in silence. Then he sighed, and turned back toward the others.

"You are right, Hoffmann." His big shoulders seemed to sag. "You are right. For us there is no other choice." Turning, Walther walked slowly back to the table, floor boards creaking under his weight. "But how can we do it? How can we capture Daring's girl?"

Hoffmann glanced quickly at the two Africans, but his face showed no emotion whatever. Then he looked up at the big man in khaki. "Daring's kids and their friend are planning to canoe downriver this Monday. We will intercept them."

Walther's thick face showed surprise. "How did you learn that?"

"Erickson told me. The trip was planned before he had to escape." Reaching into the brown leather brief-case on the floor beside his chair, he pulled out a tattered map. He spread it on the table and traced his finger along the line of the river. Where the river forked, Hoffmann stabbed with his forefinger. "We will meet them here!"

At the other end of the valley the last two hyenas, with bellies bulging, staggered away from the ravaged carcass, licking their chops. The vultures swooped in for their prey.

CHAPTER 11

THREE CANOES

Hawkins and his daughter heard the plane before they saw it. "That's them!" he said. "Sure you don't want to go with them on the river? They invited you."

"Not this time, Dad," Ellen replied. "I promised to give the women from the village another lesson with the computer. I can't break my promise. But I told Mark I'd go the next time." She was sitting in the van; her dad stood beside her.

A tall giant of a man with a thick red beard, Hawkins ran a medical clinic here on the river. Eighteen years before, he'd come as a short-term medical missionary, bringing his family with him and planning to spend four weeks helping in the clinic. But they had fallen in love with Africa and with the work here. When the month was over, they'd returned to the U.S. only so he could sell his practice. Then they came back to Africa and had remained here ever since. His daughter, Ellen, had been a paraplegic since the age of nine. Now, neither the family nor the clinic could manage without her.

As the plane neared the landing strip where Hawkins and his daughter waited, Mark told David about Ellen. "She was thrown from a horse when she was nine, and she's been in a wheelchair ever since. But she hasn't stopped living! She handles the radio work for the up-country missionaries. In fact, she and I play chess by radio."

"She also manages the computer and all the record keeping for the clinic," Mr. Daring added, "And she teaches the local people to type and to work with the computer."

"And she's my best friend," Penny added.

"Will she ever be able to walk?" David asked.

"Probably not, not without her canes," Penny replied. "She talks to me about it. Sometimes at night she cries, she says. Then she remembers that the Lord told Paul that His strength was shown in Paul's weakness, and she knows that she can trust God in the wheelchair just as well as she could if she were standing and walking. She told me once that she would never pray as much for her family and friends if she didn't have to sit still."

"She also said that she wouldn't have learned to do so many things if she had been running around like other kids," Mark added. "She's quite a girl!"

Now they were above the landing strip. Mr. Daring brought the plane in and taxied back to where Hawkins and Ellen waited for them.

"Jim," Hawkins' big voice boomed, "you land that plane almost as well as Mark!"

"I'm working at it!" Daring laughed back as they

shook hands.

They walked over to the van where the Darings hugged Ellen and then introduced David. Her eyes were gray, David noticed, with a mischievous spark, and she had long dark hair. She shook his hand with a firm grip. Then Hawkins drove all of them the short distance to the river where the canoe was docked.

Here Penny and Ellen plunged into conversation while Hawkins, Daring, and the boys studied the map of the river.

"You know the place, Mark," Hawkins said, pointing out their route on the map. "Just avoid those southern forks, and you'll do fine. We've just checked and there're no crocodiles in the main river."

They were all aware of the danger from crocodiles. "But should one ever approach you," Hawkins added, "remember their tricks. Their favorite is to bump a canoe, tip it over, grab a man, and take him to the bottom. Or they just reach up and pull him out of the boat. Then they turn over and over until he drowns, bring the body to the beach, and eat it. So if one comes after you, shoot it! The natives here hate 'em."

"That's why I want you and David to wear the pistols," Mark's dad added. "Keep a sharp lookout—just in case!"

"We checked and the river's clear," Hawkins reassured them. "Those monsters are all in the southern forks that branch off from the river, a long way downstream. Stay away from those and you won't have any trouble." He turned and led them to the dock.

"Is that your new canoe, Dr. Hawkins?" Mark asked as they approached the boat tied to the low wooden dock.

"It is," Hawkins nodded. "Made by Old Town. It's their Penobscot 17. Weighs just sixty-nine pounds, but carries eleven hundred pounds of people and gear. The thing's got a rounded bottom for speed, but it's very stable. We love it."

They looked over the red-hulled boat with dark trim and sharp bow. "You won't have problems anywhere on the river with this boat," Hawkins told them. "And the hull is indestructible. Seventeen feet long and three feet wide. It's a great craft. Wish I could go with you," he said wistfully. Then he laughed. "But I've had fun with it already. Now it's your turn!"

The boys took the packs and the cooler from the van and put them in the canoe as Penny and Ellen said their good-byes. "I'll fly the way you're going," Mr. Daring said, "and if I see anything unusual I'll come back and drop a message by float." This was their usual agreement, although they'd never had any reason to turn back.

David and Mark checked the packs with their survival gear. They were strapping on holstered .357s just as Penny joined them. Mr. Daring meanwhile put the inflatable life belts in the canoe. All three young people wore khaki pants and shirts, with wide-brimmed hats to shield them from the sun, and Penny had her camera case. They looked like intrepid jungle explorers.

"I hope you like the river, David," Ellen said from the Land Rover. "There's so much to see."

"I do," David replied. "Actually, I'm the one who taught Mark how to handle a canoe. He was pathetic until I showed him how."

"How can you make up such tales?" Mark protested.

The three climbed into the canoe: Mark in back, David in front, and Penny in the middle. She got out her camera gear and covered it with a plastic sheet to protect if from any water spray from the paddles. They shoved off from the dock, waved, and headed out into the river.

A short while later they heard Daring's Cessna take off. He waggled his wings as he passed over them and headed downriver. Mark and David waved their paddles as he whizzed past. The plane followed the course of the water, winding and turning with it, as Daring looked carefully for trouble of any kind. But the scene was utterly peaceful. He saw no boats on the water, and only a few large tree branches floating down with the current.

Then, a considerable way downriver, Daring saw a Land Rover parked by the shore. It had racks for canoes on top, but he saw neither canoes nor any people. From habit, he marked the place in his mind and flew on. In a short while he had covered the same distance it would take the kids several hours to traverse. At the ferry landing, he turned and headed for home, assured that the young folks would be safe on the river.

Hoffmann was with the two canoes at the riverbank, hidden under the long tree branches which hung out over the water, when Daring flew over. Walther, Kala, and Mapunda were likewise hidden, not far from the Land Rover.

"That's Daring," Walther said. "He always scouts ahead when his kids are on the water, but he can't see us under these trees."

"He'll see the Land Rover, though," Kala said. Earlier, he had urged Hoffmann to hide the vehicle under the trees.

"What's a Land Rover?" Walther replied. "Everyone has them. Hunters, farmers, prospectors—who hasn't got a Land Rover?" He'd become irritated by Kala's caution.

Kala looked back at the big man through expressionless eyes. If it were not for the money, he'd have left these foreigners long ago. So confident they were, as if they could never be wrong! He didn't like their carelessness; he didn't like their arrogance; but he *did* like their cash.

Yet not at the cost of his life—or his freedom. If the foreigners endangered him, he'd leave them in an instant. He and Mapunda had already agreed on that. He picked up his paddle and headed toward the river where Hoffmann waited with the two canoes.

Hoffmann had chosen this spot with care. The tall trees covered them from the sky, and the thick bush concealed them from the road which led to the river.

When the others joined him, he reviewed his plan.

"We'll wait for them here," he said. It was hot on the river and the sweat poured down his face. "We're right across from the fork where the river branches south. That's where the crocodiles are, and everyone who uses the river hugs this side when they come to that fork. We'll wait until they are right on us. Then we'll push out and box them in. Mapunda and Walther will paddle; Kala and I will cover the boys with our rifles."

"What if they have guns?" Walther asked. "Daring's son can shoot."

"They won't have time," Hoffmann replied. "We'll have rifles on them as we come out from under the tree branches. They won't see us until we're on them. We'll order them to come close and then make the girl get in the canoe with you and Kala. They won't take any chances with our rifles on them—and on her."

"What'll we do with the boys?" Walther asked.

"Make them beach their canoe on our side of the river. We'll wreck it and leave them stranded. It'll be a day before they get picked up by another canoe. By then, we'll be far away."

Hoffmann checked his rifle, working the action and putting a bullet into the chamber. "Then we radio Schmidt that we've got the girl and let him handle it from there. We'll be hidden up-country where they'll never find us. When he radios, we'll release her and leave with a safe-conduct pass. That's the deal

Schmidt will make."

Each man sat considering the plan in his own mind. The thick tree branches which extended out over the water from the bank hid them from sight. They would wait until the kids were on them and then spring out and close the trap. There would be no warning. The plan was foolproof.

CHAPTER 12

TO THE FORKS

Mark, Penny, and David started down the river at an easy pace. They had a long day's paddling ahead and they wanted to enjoy the trip. Penny got out her notebook and pen and began writing down the time, the place, the kind of film she was using, and the general lighting conditions. She always made notes as she took pictures.

"As soon as we're out of sight of the landing, we'll start seeing more birds," she told David. He turned and looked at her as she continued. "You won't believe how many different kinds there are." Her eyes were shining with pleasure. The wide-brimmed hat framed her face and light brown hair. David wished he had a picture of her.

"She makes it sound like fun, but don't believe it, David," her brother said as they paddled. "She means to drive us like slaves. 'Over there, boys!' and 'Back to this side!' and, 'Look! Let's go across again!' This will be murder," Mark teased. He really loved to take Penny on the river.

"That's all we do in life, Mark," David agreed solemnly. "Serve, serve, serve! We're just slaves to women's whims."

Penny laughed at their nonsense as she took her binoculars out of the case, put the strap around her neck, and began to search the left bank of the river. It was still early, but the sun was high enough that she wasn't bothered by the glare from the water. The dirty, brown river moved rapidly, carrying the canoe downstream and making paddling very easy for Mark and David.

"There!" Penny cried softly, pointing to her left. Mark turned the boat, and they glided quietly in the direction she'd indicated. "That's close enough," she said. David and Mark backed their paddles carefully, keeping the canoe aimed at the birds Penny had spotted.

Putting down the binoculars she took up her camera, attached the telephoto lense, and began taking pictures. The boys took turns viewing the birds through the binoculars while Penny photographed. The canoe drifted lazily with the current, requiring only an occasional shift of Mark's paddle to keep it on course. They spoke in low voices and used Penny's bird identification book to look up the species they didn't know.

David turned to face Penny, noting how she handled the camera with practiced ease. The sun made her brown hair seem lighter in color, even blond. She was intent on her work, and he stole glances at her often, as he and Mark talked quietly.

Tall trees rose from each side of the river, while thick brush formed a dense wall that came right to the river bank. As they drifted with the current, however, they noticed breaks in the brush, and once they even saw a path.

"What's behind that brush on the bank?" David asked.

"Some very uneven ground," Mark said. "Paths, small hills, some clearings. But we avoid this territory. Too many snakes and some wild pigs—to say nothing of the insects.

Time passed pleasantly. Penny searched the banks with her binoculars as they paddled. When she found more birds to photograph, she'd ask them to row closer while she took pictures. Then they would move back to the middle of the river. David realized he was watching a serious photographer.

They drank lemonade from a plastic jug, keeping the canteens full of water for later. Since coming to Africa, the Darings had heard too many tales of people who'd perished from travelling without enough food and water. They always took plenty of both, whether going by land, air, or river.

"Look at those!" David said suddenly, pointing downstream. Penny and Mark turned swiftly and looked where he was pointing.

"Flamingos!" Mark said with awe. "Hundreds of flamingos! They're coming from the lakes, but I wonder where they're going."

David thought the bright pink birds were an amazing sight, flying across the river from right to left.

Soon they vanished behind the trees.

"Oh, I didn't have time to get those," Penny said. "What a picture they'd make, though." She turned back to the shore and resumed her careful photographing of the birds there. No one noticed the passage of time until Mark asked, "Who's hungry?"

"How can you think of your stomach all the time, Mark?" Penny replied. "Wouldn't you rather think of the scenery and the beauty of everything instead of food? Why can't you be more spiritual like David?"

"I'm spiritual and I'm starved too!" David said. "Let's eat, Mark, while Penny is enjoying the scenery and watching for birds. Somebody's got to be physical enough to paddle this spiritual girl down the river."

"Oh, well, if you boys insist, I'll join you," Penny said hastily, putting down her camera and notebook. She began to unpack the sandwiches from the cooler at her feet.

Mark let the canoe drift with the swiftly flowing current, occasionally putting in his paddle to keep their course straight as they ate a leisurely lunch.

"I just love the river," Penny said between bites. "It's so peaceful."

Suddenly David pointed to the shore. "What's that hanging from the tree, Mark?"

Mark picked up the binoculars and looked. "A python. He's wrapped around the lower branch, waiting for an animal to come down that path to the river." Mark handed the glasses to Penny, who shuddered and passed them to David.

"He'll stay there until something suitable comes by," Mark continued, "and then he'll strike. He'll drop from the tree and bite, wrap himself around his prey, and squeeze it to death. Then he'll swallow it and crawl off into the woods to digest the thing. That's why you've got to look up when you walk around here. The big ones will attack a man."

"That's also why we take the canoe and stay on the water," Penny said.

"I was going to suggest we land someplace where we can get out and stretch," David said. "But I've changed my mind!"

"Oh, we can get out," Mark said. "There's a beach on the right-hand shore, just a little way ahead. We usually pull up there for a while."

"You're sure it's safe?" David asked suspiciously.

"Well," Mark hesitated, "we can at least see anything coming at us from the woods and jump back into the canoe while Penny fights it off!"

"What chivalry!" Penny said.

David laughed. "Well, if she'll fight off anything that comes after us, I guess we can land. I sure need to stretch!"

Shortly afterward, they came to the sandy spot. About forty yards long, it extended almost twenty yards inland. They beached the canoe and got out. Penny began to photograph flowers while Mark and David looked carefully around the area. Then the boys

stretched and raced each other up and down the shore
to loosen their muscles.

They were all sweating as they got back in the
canoe and pushed off, feeling better for the exercise.
The sun was high overhead now. A lone hawk weaved
back and forth across the sky, seeming to follow the
canoe as it travelled down the river.

Suddenly David pointed his paddle to the left.
"Look! Wild pigs!"

Half a dozen of the ugly dark animals were rooting
along the river bank. As the boat came closer, the three
voyagers could hear the deadly creatures grunting and
puffing.

"They're dangerous," Mark said soberly. "They're
not big, but if they knock you down they'll rip you up
with their teeth and tusks. And they're fast! That's
another reason we carry pistols in country like this."

"Oh, you're always talking about danger, Mark,"
Penny scolded. "Why don't you forget about those
things and enjoy yourself? Sometimes you're so
gloomy."

She picked up her binoculars and looked down the
river, searching for a species of bird she called *turacos*.

"Speaking of danger," Mark said, "it's time we
moved over to the other side. We're getting close to
where the river forks—the left branch leads to where
the crocodiles hang out. We always move over to the
right just in case."

He turned his paddle sideways, and the canoe

angled to the right as David plunged his paddle deep and gave a powerful thrust. They came closer to the right-hand shore, which was thick with brush and tall trees. Some of the tree branches hung far out over the river. The boys paddled leisurely while Penny scouted the shore line, looking for birds.

A fast-moving stream entered the river to their right, and David noted that the current was moving more quickly now. Then, ahead and on the left, he saw the fork in the river.

"Is that it?" David asked, pointing across the wide river. "Is that the fork that leads to the crocodiles?"

"That's it," Mark answered. The boys looked intently at the widening branch of the river as their canoe moved more rapidly downstream. "Sure looks peaceful enough to me," David said.

"It is. We just like to make sure we've got lots of room in case we happen to see anything we want to get away from," Mark chuckled. "Nothing will bother us on this side."

Suddenly Penny put down her binoculars. "Mark," she said in a hushed tone, "there are two canoes hiding under tree branches about a hundred yards ahead."

Mark plunged his paddle into the water behind and to the left, then shoved it forward, spinning the canoe into a turn. "Paddle hard on the right side, David," he said urgently. "You do the same, Penny."

David drove his paddle into the water in a long, powerful sweep. Penny grabbed the extra paddle stored under her seat, waited for David's stroke, and then plunged her blade into the water.

The canoe completed its sudden turn and headed upstream. Mark, at the stern, pulled with powerful strokes, aiming the canoe back at a sharp angle to cross the river. His strokes at the rear had more effect than David's and Penny's.

The canoe sped upriver, slicing back against the current at a forty-five-degree angle and, they hoped, hidden from the men waiting under the long branches.

CHAPTER 13

PURSUED

Hoffman climbed down from the branch where he'd been perched. Putting his binoculars into their case, he dropped into the front of the canoe; Mapunda sat in the back. Walther and Kala were in the canoe alongside.

"Here they come!" Hoffmann said in low tones. "They're crossing the river to our side. It won't be long now. Remember, we'll wait until they're here, then dash out in front of them. Mapunda and I will go to the far side of their boat; Kala and Walther will box them in on this side. They'll be trapped between our two canoes and we'll cover them with the rifles."

He was pleased with the simplicity of his plan. "The boys won't dare do a thing. We'll order the girl to get in your canoe," he said to Kala. "Then we'll move the boys between us to the shore. When they get out, we'll sink their canoe with our hatchets, take the girl with us in the Land Rover, and radio Schmidt. He'll contact Daring and demand the claim papers in exchange for her release. Any questions?"

There were none. Hoffmann sat in the bow of Mapunda's canoe, peering through an opening in the branches that drooped to the surface of the river. He could spot the kids just before they came abreast of their position. They waited.

And waited.

No one came. Hoffmann fidgeted nervously, wondering what was causing the delay. He looked at his watch again. Finally he could stand it no longer.

"What's keeping those kids? Push out a bit, Mapunda, so I can see the river. Just a little way."

Mapunda put his paddle in the water and eased the canoe a few feet forward. Hoffmann leaned lower, peering through the low-hanging branches. Suddenly, he jerked upright, his face red with anger.

"They're going back across the river!" he said hotly.

"They must have seen us," Kala said, glancing darkly at Mapunda. Nothing about this business had gone according to plan.

"Let's go!" Hoffmann yelled. "We'll head straight across the river. That way, we'll cut them off if they turn back downstream. They can't hope to escape us if they're going upriver. And they can't go toward the crocodiles. We've still got them trapped!"

The two canoes shot out into the river and headed across to the other shore. Now they all saw the kids' canoe moving very quickly to their left, angling back upstream.

Meanwhile, Mark, David, and Penny, paddling with all their strength, had covered twenty yards, then thirty, then forty. Now they were at midstream and moving fast.

Mark glanced back as he finished a stroke. No sign of pursuit. They were closing on the other shore. He looked back again; still the ambushers had not come out.

"David, you and Penny paddle on the left side. We'll turn and angle downriver. We may get past them before they know what we're doing."

But it was too late! Even as the young people turned downstream, the two canoes on the other side came into view, heading to cut them off!

"Paddle as hard as you can," Mark said, digging his blade into the water while David and Penny did likewise. Their strokes drove the swift boat rapidly downstream with the current. Mark angled them closer to the far shore.

Downriver, the pursuers saw their change of course. "They're heading downstream again!" Kala called.

"Cut right," Hoffmann ordered urgently. "We can still head them off."

Instantly the two canoes turned farther to the right, angling downriver. The four strong men drove their paddles smoothly into the swift-moving water.

"We'll be cut off," David said to Mark between strokes. "They've got the angle on us."

Without interrupting his strokes, Mark glanced up anxiously. David was right! Penny said nothing. She paddled smoothly, in unison with David. They were all kneeling now, for greater stability and power in their strokes.

"Turn left, Mark!" David yelled suddenly. "There's a floating log ahead of us."

Desperately, Mark turned his blade. The canoe rocked and swerved to the left, directly toward the river fork they'd sought to avoid.

They barely missed the huge half-submerged tree trunk. As soon as they passed it, Mark turned back downstream. The three paddled as hard as they could to escape the closing trap. Ahead and to their right were the two pursuing canoes. Ahead and to their left was the fork that might lead to crocodiles. They had to get past those canoes!

Mark glanced again at the other two canoes. "Hey, that's Hoffmann and Walther, the men Dad showed us at the airport!"

David looked at the position of the canoes to their right. "They're going to head us off, Mark," David said again, with urgency in his voice. "We've got to take the left fork!"

Mark knew they had no other choice. "You're right. They're heading us off." His voice was grim.

Now the mouth of the river's fork opened to their left. "Slow down a bit," Mark said softly, knowing how far loud voices carry over water. "We'll keep heading downriver till the last moment, then we'll cut left. Maybe that big branch hanging over the river ahead of us will keep them from seeing that we've turned, at least for a minute."

The three eased up on their strokes; the boat was

still flying through the muddy water.

Just when they were about to pass the fork, Mark said with quiet urgency, "Paddle on the right! I'm turning now!"

He drove his paddle deep in the water, spinning the canoe to the left and scraping low-hanging branches from the shore. David and Penny paddled furiously, and the canoe shot down the course that led to the beach of crocodiles.

The large tree branch that hung out over the water shielded their sudden turn from the two canoes that paddled to head them off against the river bank. For a minute, the men didn't notice their change of course. Kala was the first to call out.

"They're gone!" he yelled.

All four men stopped paddling and looked upriver, searching for the youngsters with anxious eyes. The canoes still coasted rapidly from the power of their paddling.

"Are they hiding in those low branches?" Walther asked sharply.

"I don't think so," Kala said. "I think they turned down that fork."

"But the crocodiles are down there," Walther retorted angrily. "Why would they do such a stupid thing?"

"Because they had no other choice," Kala replied. When would this European learn that people would not always do as he wished them to? Again he glanced at Mapunda, who returned his gaze.

"We'll head back!" Hoffmann snapped. "We've still got them boxed in!"

Mapunda and Walther in the stern of their boats turned their blades, Kala and Hoffmann paddled hard, and the canoes spun to the left and headed upriver. "Faster!" Hoffmann called. "We've got to make sure they don't get out." The four men paddled with all their power against the swift current.

"Don't forget that Daring's kid may have a pistol," Walther called over to Hoffmann as the two canoes streaked swiftly through the water.

"But we've got rifles, man! He won't try anything against our rifles—not with his sister with him. We've got them now!" Hoffmann exulted.

CHAPTER 14

CROCODILE BEACH

"Let's rest for a minute," Mark said.

Their shirts were soaked with sweat. Their faces showed full awareness of the danger they faced. They'd swept through the entrance to the river's left branch, followed its curving path, and then paddled hard for another fifty yards. It was time to take a short break, Mark thought, before they wore themselves out. They had a good head start on their pursuers; those men would have to paddle back against the current before they could turn down this fork to continue the chase. That would give them a workout!

Mark got off his knees and sat on the seat, keeping his paddle in the water to stay them on course. The splendid boat still moved quickly, the swift current adding to its speed.

David turned and sat on the front seat, facing the other two. "That was great work, Penny. You spotted those boats just in time." He wiped the sweat from his face with his sleeve. "That's the second time you've saved us from being ambushed!"

She smiled her thanks, her face lighting for a moment. Then she frowned. "But why are they chasing us?" she asked anxiously. "What do they want?"

She too got up from her knees, turned, and sat on the seat facing her brother. Her knees were sore from kneeling, and her arms ached from paddling so long and hard. It was a relief to sit for a minute. Again she asked, "What can they want with us?"

"I've been thinking about that," Mark said, equally worried. "Maybe they want to use us as a ransom, to make Dad give up the mining rights we took to the Nairobi. Dad says that they really want that diamond mine." Mark's eyes were clouded with concern. "We never thought they'd go to such lengths, though." He looked at David behind Penny's head; the two boys were alarmed that Penny was in danger.

"But if they kidnap us, they must know that they'll be in trouble with the law," Penny said. "Dad told us that the men you two caught in that shed near Mboto may *never* get out of jail for kidnapping Mr. Rush." Her brown eyes were troubled as she searched for an explanation.

"Mark," she said suddenly, "they must be desperate if they're taking such chances. We've got to escape, haven't we?"

"You're right," Mark replied honestly, looking into her eyes. Again he glanced past her and looked at David. The boys knew that her safety depended on them.

"We'll get away," David said with grim determination. Mark nodded agreement as he moved the boat with a few strong strokes, then rested his arms again.

This part of the river was only forty yards across, with trees and brush identical to what they'd been seeing all day. A dark green wall seemed to hem the river in on either side. There was no breeze, and the heat was greater than on the main channel. But the water was the same dirty brown, and it was moving quickly, carrying the canoe with it while the paddlers rested. There were occasional tree branches in the water and the three kept careful watch. They didn't want to get snagged or capsized by one of those!

"Let's check the map and see what's ahead," Mark said grimly. He took it from his pack, spread it out between him and Penny, and studied it intently. Then he handed it to his sister. "You two look at this while I paddle. We can't stop moving." He began paddling with powerful, even strokes, and the canoe picked up speed while Penny turned and studied the map with David.

"See how far we go before we get to the crocodiles," Mark said. "There are beaches on both sides of the river there, with a narrow island between them. The crocs are supposed to hang out on the right bank."

Penny and David studied the map between them. "I think we have a mile, or a mile and a half to go," she said.

David agreed. "This branch bends back to the right until it heads straight away from the main channel.

Then it curves right again and parallels the river we were on. When we come around that curve we'll be in sight of the island and the beaches."

He looked at the map again. "I don't see any path on either side or any other beach. But could we land and head inland through the bush? We could push the canoe downstream so they couldn't tell where we'd gone ashore."

"I don't think so," Mark replied. "You don't know how thick that bush is. We'd have to fight our way through that stuff, not knowing where we were going, and they could easily see where we'd tramped through. I think they'd catch us in no time. We can go faster on the river, at least for now."

Then he spoke the grim thought that was in all their minds: "But now we've got to watch for crocodiles all the time."

"Right," David said resignedly. He turned around, knelt again, and began adding his strokes to Mark's. Penny did the same. The three of them paddled in silence, constantly looking ahead and to the side. The canoe sped forward.

Then Mark remembered something. "Doesn't the map show a path leading away from the left-hand beach ahead of us? See if you can find that, Penny." His voice had a note of hope.

Penny picked up the map as Mark and David paddled with long, strong strokes. They knew they had to conserve strength as well as stay ahead of their pursuers.

The good design of the canoe was serving them well.

"There is a path, just across from the island!" she said. "But then it disappears in the bush. It must lead somewhere, but the map doesn't show where." She started paddling again, wondering how a path that simply ended could help them.

The river curved more than the map had indicated. Long tree branches reached out from each bank, preventing Mark from seeing very far behind him when he looked back. As yet, there was no sign of pursuit. The other canoes were nowhere in sight, nor could they be so soon, he knew. But they were back there somewhere.

They were indeed. With Hoffmann goading them, the men had turned their boats and paddled urgently into the river current, heading directly upstream. The two craft were so close to each other that when Kala suddenly yelled "Tree ahead!" and pointed with his paddle, Walther's swift change of direction from the stern sent the two canoes crashing into each other.

Hoffmann went overboard with a yell, losing his paddle in the fall. Both canoes crashed into the low-lying branches of the great tree that spread out from the bank, and the three men struggled violently to back out. Finally, they freed the boats and turned to get Hoffmann, who was treading water frantically.

Mapunda grabbed Hoffmann and hauled the spluttering man into the canoe. The river's dirty water poured from his sodden clothes. In the other canoe, Kala and Walther found Hoffman's floating paddle and brought it to him. Mapunda and Kala couldn't help grinning at the dripping man, who was now in a towering rage at the delay.

"They'll have a huge lead on us," he yelled.

"Not when they spot those crocodiles, they won't," Mapunda said grimly.

The two crafts skirted the giant tree branches and again began heading upstream.

The men were strong and skillful, but paddling so hard and fast against the river was gruelling. When they came to the entrance of the river's fork and turned to follow the young people, they were exhausted.

Here the enraged Hoffmann came to his senses. "Slow down," he called out. "They can't escape us now. Let's not kill ourselves paddling."

They slowed to an easier pace. But their anger knew no bounds at the trouble these young people were giving them.

Just then Kala called over to Hoffmann. "Wait! Look at those long tree branches hanging over the water from the shore. If they hid under those branches, we would not see them as we passed."

Hoffmann thought about this. "You're right, Kala." He looked at the thick trees on either side of the river with their long branches under which a canoe could easily hide. "Let's go in column. You and Walther go ahead and search those branches as you pass. If they try to hide, you'll spot them, and we'll have them boxed between us."

Kala nodded approvingly at Hoffmann's show of reason. He and Walther pulled ahead of the other canoe. Now the two boats were in single file. The men searched the banks on each side as they paddled.

"This will slow us down, though," Walther said.

"What's the rush?" Hoffmann asked sarcastically. "They'll have to stop before they get to the crocodiles. Then we'll have them."

"The crocodiles will have us all if we get too close," Mapunda growled. "There are many of them, and we wouldn't be able to shoot them all before they tip us over."

Mapunda had grown up in a village along a river filled with the beasts. As a boy, he'd known men who'd been killed by crocodiles. Their boats had been attacked, and the men dragged under and drowned, then eaten later by the fierce amphibians. He feared these animals immensely.

"We won't have to get that close," Hoffmann snapped confidently. "We'll let the crocs scare the kids back to us. They'll have no choice."

The brush on each side was thick. Birds flitted among trees, their sharp cries shattering the air. Once the men heard wild pigs rooting and grunting along the shore, but they couldn't see them.

"I think the men in front should keep their rifles ready and let us paddle," Mapunda said suddenly. "If that boy came out suddenly with his pistol on us, we'd be helpless."

Everyone realized at once that he was right. Hoffmann put down his paddle and picked up his rifle. Kala, in the other boat, did the same. Mapunda and Walther kept the canoes moving with powerful strokes.

Ahead of them half a mile, and completely out of sight behind the turns in the river, Mark, Penny, and David were fast approaching the lair of the crocodiles.

"David, I think you should trade places with Penny and have your gun ready. You can paddle if we need you to, but you'd be able to shoot better from the middle of the boat."

"Right," David replied, grim at the prospect of trying to shoot attacking crocodiles from a moving canoe.

He and Penny squeezed by each other as they swapped places, careful not to tip the boat. While she knelt in front and paddled, Mark and David drew their pistols and checked the loads. David took out the plastic case from his pack, removed six shells, and put these in his shirt pocket for quick reloading; Mark did the same. Then they both resumed paddling.

"Remember," Mark said, "watch for signs of their bodies under the water. The crocs like to hit a boat and tip it over. They'll also grab an arm and pull you in. We want to shoot them before they reach us. And we want to stay low so we can't be knocked out of the canoe."

"Let's ask the Lord to help us," David said. While Mark steered, David asked God to protect them from the animals ahead. Then Penny did the same. Mark concluded, "Oh, Father, make us know what to do. Please guide us. Keep us safe. We ask in Jesus' name. Amen."

When they finished praying, David had another thought. "Remember to shoot low, Mark. These high-powered bullets climb when they leave the barrel."

"You're right," Mark answered, "but maybe we won't have to shoot. If we're quiet, I'm hoping we can pass those animals without their noticing. Look for them on the right side—that's where they're supposed to hang out. Then we can hug the left bank. If we let the current carry us past them so we don't make noise paddling, they might not notice us before that island comes between us," he said hopefully. "If we can just reach that island, we'll be hidden from their sight. Then we can glide right by them. They usually sleep in the sun."

They paddled farther and came to the last bend of the river before the beaches.

"O.K., gang, this is it," David said. "Now we'll know if they're there or not."

They came around the curve in the river, staring anxiously ahead as the two beaches came into view. The narrow island split the channel before them and the dirty river water flowed quickly past it on either side. Behind them, four angry men pursued. What was ahead?

CHAPTER 15

THE JAWS OF DEATH

"**S**ound carries over water," Mark reminded them in a whisper. He paddled only enough to steer.

David picked up Penny's binoculars as they rounded the bend and studied the left bank of the river. Mark and Penny waited anxiously for his report. Sweat rolled off his face into his eyes, and he had to brush it away to see through the lenses.

"There's the beach," he whispered. "I don't see any animals on that one."

"How about the other side?" Mark asked.

David turned to the right and studied the shore. His jaw muscles tightened. Putting the binoculars down he turned, looked bleakly at Mark, and said quietly, "It's covered with crocs."

"How many?" Mark asked. Then quickly, "Never mind! I'll steer across to the other side. Penny, don't paddle at all. You two just sit low in the boat and stay still. Maybe they'll think we're a tree branch or a log—or something," he said hopefully.

Mark stopped paddling and simply steered the boat across the river, heading to the left of the island ahead. Their momentum and the current kept them moving. With hearts pounding furiously the three scanned the beach on the right. Now Penny and Mark could see the tangle of crocodiles lying on the sand, sunning themselves.

Penny found that she was holding her breath! Deliberately, she made herself breathe again as the canoe drew closer to the left shore. The island in the middle of the river loomed nearer. Really just a narrow piece of sand, it was covered with low bush and a few small trees.

Penny felt as if they were in a slow-motion film where everything took too long to happen. The current did move, however, and it brought them closer to the left-hand beach. She felt her heart pounding and hoped the crocodiles couldn't hear it! They were getting close to the spot where the island would shield them from the big beasts on the other side.

Mark's steering had brought them near the shore where tree branches towered high above them, sometimes shielding them from the sun so that the boat moved through patches of shadow on the river.

"Maybe they won't see us in these shadows!" David whispered.

Penny nodded.

"At least they're not moving," Mark added.

But just then, one of the crocodiles swung his mas-

sive head in their direction. The young people held
their breath! Mark kept steering, however, and the current moved them closer and closer to the place where
the island would block them from the deadly animals
on the far shore. Just a few more yards!

"We're almost there!" Mark said quietly as he
looked across. "If they don't see us now, we can get
past them before they know it."

"Mark!" Penny cried suddenly. "There's a big
branch under water, right in front of us!"

Mark plunged his paddle into the water, swerving
the craft away from the large branch but directly
toward the crocodiles across the channel. The submerged branch scraped the side of their canoe with a
screeching sound that carried across the water.

Immediately past the branch, Mark turned the
canoe sharply back to the left—but it was too late!

More crocodiles were turning their heads towards
them, apparently startled by the commotion they'd
made. Suddenly, one darted toward the water with
incredible speed.

"Paddle, both of you!" Mark yelled. "We've got to
get to shore! We'll climb those rocks at the edge of the
bush. They can't reach us there!"

David and Penny drove their paddles into the water
and the boat leaped ahead, speeding toward the empty
beach behind which a cluster of rocks rose under the
tall trees. *We're still forty yards away*, David thought.

The first crocodile launched itself into the river and

disappeared from sight. A second did the same. Then Mark's anguished eyes saw at least ten of the giant amphibians race to the water. Large splashes convulsed the water by the shore where the animals plunged in, as if a battery of field artillery had opened up on the spot.

"Paddle!" Mark called. "We've got to beat them to the shore!"

The canoe skimmed across the water, driven by the three desperate teens. But Mark saw patches of swirling water, disturbed by swimming crocodiles below, coming rapidly closer.

"David," he yelled, "get ready to shoot! Both of you stay as low as you can."

Mark and Penny paddled with all their might as David, crouched low in the middle of the canoe, put down his paddle and drew his revolver. He turned carefully and knelt facing back toward the approaching crocodiles, eyes searching the water behind and on either side. If they could just reach the shore ahead of the pursuing animals!

They didn't make it. David saw the water move to his left, and the large ugly head of a crocodile broke the surface just ten feet away from the side of the canoe. Holding the powerful pistol in both hands, he pulled back the hammer with his thumb, aimed deliberately down the animal's throat and squeezed the trigger as the mighty jaws opened in front of him. The big gun bucked in his hand with a terrific sound!

Penny screamed with surprise, but kept paddling. The stricken animal turned with incredible swiftness back to his left, shaking the boat violently as he went under and behind them.

Penny and Mark lurched forward, but righted themselves by gripping the sides of the boat. David fell sideways and his arm went in the water. He wrenched himself back, still gripping the gun in his other hand.

"Paddle, Penny!" Mark yelled.

Just then David saw another long shape heading directly for the boat. He raised his gun, but the animal suddenly turned and streaked for the wounded crocodile behind them. The water exploded as the injured animal broke the surface, twisting frantically to escape. The second crocodile had clamped its long jaws around the neck of the wounded one. Its victim was rolling over and over, trying to throw off its attacker, spraying water for yards. Another crocodile attacked the already wounded one, and now three of them were tearing the surface of the river to foam.

But there were more! The boat suddenly tipped upward from the middle, and the three young people grabbed for balance. Penny's paddle flew out of her hands and into the water. David had both hands on the pistol as he crashed against the side of rhe boat Looking frantically to his right as he recovered his balance, he saw the back half of the huge animal as it scraped the bottom of their canoe, rocking them all again. Twisting to his left, he saw the large head above the surface. David fired. Quickly he fired again.

The animal went berserk, twisting completely over, hitting the boat again before plunging desperately into the depths of the river.

"Paddle, Penny!" Mark yelled again, as he drove his blade into the water with all his strength. They had to reach the shore and run to those rocks!

Penny almost fell backwards as she twisted to reach the paddle that David had put down. She got one hand on it, struggled back to her place, and began paddling frantically once more. The canoe picked up speed as another violent fight occurred behind and to their left. The crocodile David had just hit burst to the surface, locked in the jaws of another amphibian. Twisting round and round, the wounded animal sought desperately to shake its assailant.

"David! Ahead of us!" Penny screamed.

David turned to the front of the boat as an immense crocodile hit them from straight ahead. Penny fell forward into the boat as the canoe tipped to the right. Mark did the same, then lunged frantically back as the crocodile's jaws came toward him, its narrow eyes just a few feet away, its foul breath choking him.

David kept his balance this time and fired twice into the skull of the huge animal only three feet away from his gun.

The crocodile simply stopped swimming and slowly sank. Mark and Penny, shaken, began paddling again.

"Penny," Mark yelled, "when the boat touches bottom, jump out and run. Take your pack! David, I'll run the canoe up on the beach. Cover me. Then we'll get our packs and run for the rocks."

The canoe scraped sand. Penny leaped out, her pack and binoculars in one hand, camera case in the other. David and Mark jumped out, splashed into the shallow water, and followed her onto the beach. Mark ran the canoe on the shore.

David whirled around, searching the shore line frantically as he backed toward the others, conscious that he had only one shot left in the gun.

"Come on, David!" Mark yelled. "Grab your pack!"

David scooped up his pack from the canoe as he ran by. Penny was ahead of him, climbing the rocks. Mark was backing toward her, pack in one hand, leveled gun in the other, pointing toward the water.

Both boys reached the rocks just as a large crocodile erupted from the river and flew toward them across the sand. David lined his sights on the rushing monster thinking it incredible that something that looked so awkward could move so fast!

Mark fired first, but the animal kept coming. Both boys aimed carefully at the terrifying creature and squeezed off a shot carefully when it was just a few feet away.

"Hurry! Hurry!" Penny called frantically. She was halfway up the rocks now and safe.

The crocodile went wild, twisting in circles, then streaking across the beach and plunging madly into the river. David and Mark holstered their guns and scrambled up the rocks to join Penny on a ledge. Here they turned to look at the beach.

The boys reloaded their pistols as they watched the fight. The vicious animals broke above the surface and plunged under again as they attacked each other in a frenzy. Mark counted three fights at least, maybe more. They saw single crocodiles glide across the surface, then plunge under the turbulent waters to join the fray below.

"That was great shooting, David!" Mark said.

"That was great paddling you two did, especially after they hit the boat," David answered.

Both boys looked at Penny with sudden seriousness. Her brother spoke their thoughts. "You've got to be the bravest girl in Africa. You were wonderful!" She blushed at her brother's praise. She didn't know what to say to the two who had just fought so magnificently to escape their pursuers and then the crocodiles. She took a deep breath and grinned. For the first time in a long while, the boys grinned back!

"We'd better get out of here," David said. "Those men might make it through like we did. And we don't know what's in the jungle ahead."

"I'm afraid you're right," Mark agreed. "Let's move! The only way is to take the path shown on the map."

The three of them struggled to put their packs on their shoulders and then climbed down the other side of the rocks. They saw the path at once, heading straight into the thick bush and directly away from the river. Mark led, Penny followed, and David brought up the rear.

"Don't forget those wild pigs we saw earlier." David kept his gun in hand as he said this. Mark did the same. The three wondered how they'd see wild pigs in time to shoot—the brush was so thick and close!

They began walking rapidly but quietly along the narrow path under the tall trees. Here it was much darker. Patches of light broke through the shadows of the leaves, but their eyes had to adjust after the glare on the river surface.

"What's that?" Penny asked suddenly, stopping. They all turned back toward the shore. Through the trees, they heard the sounds of three muffled shots.

"Those guys found our crocodiles," David said grimly.

"I hope so," Mark replied. "I can't think that they'll get this far, now that those animals are fighting in the river between us, but we can't be sure. Let's cover as much distance as we can and look for another trail. This is too obvious."

They heard the rifle fire again as they moved rapidly up the gently sloping path, which curved a bit to the right as it climbed. Then there was only the sound of their footsteps—and the birds and animals in the bush.

As they walked, each began to feel the seriousness of their plight. They were isolated and they were lost. They didn't dare go back to the river, but they didn't know where they were headed. And Mr. Daring was expecting to meet them at the river landing in three hours!

They knew they couldn't make it.

CHAPTER 16

LOST IN THE FOREST

Mr. Daring was troubled, and at first he wasn't sure why. After flying down the river ahead of the kids and seeing that it was clear, he'd flown home and plunged into the work that awaited him in the office. He was busy for several hours, studying reports from the field, calling some of the men for details, making arrangements for a team to follow up the research Tom Rush had developed in the new mining area.

But he couldn't forget the Land Rover that he'd seen after he'd left the kids. Where were the canoes that went on those racks, he wondered? And where were the people?

He ate his lunch at the office, still working on the projects at hand. Finally, nagged by worry, he called Colonel Lamumba and asked if they'd found the men who'd tried to stop the kids on the road.

"They've dropped out of sight," the Colonel replied. "We have no trace of them, and frankly, this worries me. We captured their station wagon in the city, but their Land Rover escaped somehow and we haven't located it. Hoffmann and Walther are still at large, and there are some Africans with them."

Daring thanked him and hung up. That did it! His mind was made up. He called the hangar. "Ed, get the plane ready for me, will you? I'm leaving right away to go and pick up the kids."

"Fine, Jim," Ed replied. "It'll be ready."

Daring called his wife and told her he'd be leaving a bit early. Then he went to the hangar, checked out the Cessna, and took off, setting course directly for the spot where he'd seen the Land Rover. He planned to start there and follow the river to the landing where the kids would arrive. He could land at the strip by the ferry and pick them up.

Back on the river, Hoffmann and his men had heard the pistol shots ahead of them. Kala and Walther slowed their boat, allowing Hoffmann and Mapunda to come alongside.

"They've found the crocodiles," Mapunda said grimly. "They'll be lucky to escape with their lives."

"Hurry, then!" Hoffmann cried. "They'll be coming back this way!"

They put their backs into the paddling, caution forgotten as they raced down the river. But they were a good distance behind the three youngsters, and it was some time before they reached the curve in the river that would lead them to the beaches. As they rounded the curve, Mapunda warned them, "We can't get too close if those crocodiles are in the water or we'll all be killed."

"We won't let that happen, Mapunda," Hoffmann replied with a sardonic smile. "We'll shoot them before they get close. But if we want the diamond mines, we've got to have that girl for a hostage. So paddle!"

Paddle they did, with all their might. Finally they approached the bend. "Keep your guns ready!" Hoffmann warned. "We'll likely find those kids racing this way." He seemed oblivious to the danger posed by the crocodiles, Mapunda noted with a mixture of fear and anger.

The two canoes raced around the bend of the river and headed downstream. The men were so intent on searching the beach to their right that they did not at first notice the turbulence in the river ahead. Mapunda spotted it first.

"Look out!" he called. "Crocodiles in the water!"

But there was little they could do. Their speed was so great and the force of the current so strong, that they were carried close to the underwater warfare before they could slow their course.

Kala was the first to stop paddling and pick up his rifle. Kneeling in the canoe, he fired once, twice, three times and hit one of the twisting animals in the river ahead.

"What are you doing, you fool?" Hoffmann yelled.

"Keep paddling." He dug his blade into the water and drove the boat closer to the spot where Kala had shot. Too late, he realized his danger.

The maddened wounded beast turned from the crocodile he was fighting and darted toward Hoffmann's canoe. Hoffmann dropped his paddle, picked up his rifle, and fired; Mapunda shot at the same time. The animal had submerged, however, and the shots ricocheted off the water.

The next moment their canoe was struck violently from below. Hoffmann went over the side with a yell of terror. Mapunda fell partly into the water, but caught himself and reached for the German who had come to the surface yelling with fright. For the second time that day the big African grabbed the terrified man and hauled him into the boat—just ahead of the crocodile's jaws! The canoe was struck again, and both men fell to their faces.

Kala and Walther were firing now. The water on both sides of their canoe was torn by fighting crocodiles. Wounded animals struggled to escape their vicious comrades; unwounded ones attacked all they found; and all turned and splashed with violent speed and deadly intent. It was absolute chaos—lethal chaos!

"Turn back!" Kala yelled. "It's our only chance."

Walther threw down his rifle and picked up his paddle, turning the boat while Kala continued shooting. In the other canoe, Mapunda grabbed his paddle and yelled to Hoffmann, "You shoot, I'll paddle!" The canoes spun around as the big men in the back of each took over, while the men in front fired into the water at the frenzied beasts.

They began to pull away. Gradually, the canoes moved upstream and away from the deadly struggles.

At last they reached the main course of the river and began to paddle to the spot where they'd left the Land Rover. They'd been paddling at top speed for far too long and were all thoroughly exhausted. Hoffmann was enraged at their failure to capture Penny.

Then they heard a plane!

"Quick, under the trees!" Hoffmann yelled.

The men paddled frantically to the far shore and under the long tree branches that hung over the water. They grabbed these and held the canoes still, hidden from the sky. Just in time!

Daring flew low over the place where he'd spotted the Rover. It was still there, but he saw no people. He circled lower still, using his binoculars to search the ground beneath the thickly leaved branches of the trees. He saw nothing—no men, no boats. Nothing.

Frustrated, he turned downriver and followed its course, hoping to see the kids in their canoe. On and on he flew, until he reached the ferry landing where they'd planned to meet. The air strip was just inland, but he ignored it and flew low over the landing, searching for the canoe.

He saw no signs of it, nor of the kids.

Now he was really worried. He flew back upriver,

back to the place where the Rover had been parked. It was gone! The road was covered in so many places by trees that he tried to follow it only a little way before returning to the river. But here he saw no sign of the kids and their canoe.

He radioed Colonel Lamumba and described the situation. "I'm going back to look for the kids. Can you have that Land Rover picked up?"

"We'll do that right away, Jim!" the colonel said.

Daring signed off. There was only one place left to search. With a sinking heart he turned down the river branch that led to the beaches, the one place the kids had been warned not to approach. And, in a short while, he saw crocodiles fighting in the water and others fighting on one shore. But across the river, on the other beach, he saw the canoe! It was drawn up on the sand, five yards from the water.

That was done on purpose, he said to himself. But where were the kids? There was no sign of a road in the thick bush below.

Nor were there other canoes. Turning, he flew low over the beach, which was covered with fighting crocodiles.

What in the world has happened? he asked himself.

Flying back over the canoe, he searched the ground and saw a faint indication of a trail leading away from the beach. But it soon disappeared under the thick trees. Still, it was all he had to go on. He turned the plane in that direction, flying low, weaving back and forth, searching for a break in the trees so that he could see the ground below.

Just then he spotted a stone-covered hill in a clearing. He circled it, wondering and hoping.

In the jungle beneath, the three youngsters heard the plane and stopped.

"That's Dad!" Penny cried. "That's his plane!"

"I think you're right," her brother replied, grinning with excitement. "He's found us! Thank the Lord!"

"But he can't land in this," David said, looking around at the thick underbrush beneath the tall trees.

"He sure can't," Mark said, "but at least we can let him know we're here." Hurriedly he took off his pack, took out a flare, and fired it into the sky through a break in the trees.

The brilliant light shot up from the jungle just to the left of the plane. Daring whooped with joy, turned, and circled slowly, closer and closer to the trees. Another flare shot up, and he knew it was the kids. He circled them again, then headed toward the rocky hill ahead of them. Returning, he circled again, and again headed straight towards the hill.

Below, they noticed the direction of his flight.

"He's leading us," Mark said. "Let's keep going. He's seen something we can't see through this brush."

They pushed on, following the noise of the plane above them, scrambling along the narrow trail. Finally, they saw the rocky hill ahead. Bursting through the bush, they ran up the hill, shouting and waving at the plane.

Daring flew low and waved out the window. Circling, he called Colonel Lamumba again.

"I'll send a helicopter right away," the colonel promised. "You stay there so it can find you. We'll get your people."

Daring thanked him, signed off, and wrote a quick note for the youngsters below. He stuck this in a heavy message pouch, flew low over the hill, and tossed it out the window.

The three below yelled with joy and ran to get the pouch. Mark picked it up, ripped open the tape and read the message: "Stay where you are," Daring had written. "A helicopter is on the way."

They waved back in great relief, then watched the plane begin to fly around in a wide circle. That's when they started to realize how exhausted they were! Dropping their packs to the ground, the boys holstered their pistols—no need for these anymore!

They whooped with relief. Penny threw her arms around her brother in a big hug. Then she turned to David, her eyes shining. But suddenly, her hands flew to her face. "Oh, I must look awful!"

Her clothes were sopping wet from river water and sweat, and her hair was matted and straggly. But as David looked at her he spoke the absolute truth: "Penny, you're beautiful!"

Totally surprised, she looked in his eyes for a moment and realized that he meant what he said. Joyfully, she threw her arms around his neck. He hugged her in return. Mark grinned at him over Penny's shoulder, gave a broad wink, and raised his clasped hands in silent approval.

Grunting and snarling with anger, the wild pig shot from the jungle, knocked Mark's feet from under him, and ploughed into the bush before turning for another charge. Mark crashed to the ground, stunned and utterly helpless.

Startled by Penny's sudden scream, the hairy beast swung his massive head from side to side, searching for her with angry, nearsighted eyes. Penny ran and knelt by the side of her prostrate brother.

The savage pig's dark sides heaved with his breathing, his deadly tusks gleamed with menace. He charged!

CHAPTER 17

THE DEADLY TUSKS

David whirled and drew his pistol. He was shocked at the sight before him. Mark was on the ground, Penny was kneeling beside him, and the wild pig was about to charge.

David knelt quickly and aimed his gun, tracking the animal as it moved from his left to his right, squeezing off carefully. The pistol bucked in his hand and the charging animal was knocked to the ground by the heavy slug. It didn't move, and David ran to help Penny get Mark to his feet.

"Are you all right, Mark?" Penny cried.

He held his hand to his head; there was blood where he'd hit a rock. "I think so," he answered. "What happened?"

"A wild pig rushed us from the bush there," she replied, pointing.

"We've got to move," David said urgently. "Those animals run in packs! Let's climb these rocks. We'll be safer there."

They helped Mark stand erect, and Penny handed him his pack. The three of them rushed for the rocks, Mark and Penny leading, David coming behind and watching the bush. Just as Penny and Mark began to climb, they heard fierce grunting in the jungle behind them.

"Climb!" David yelled as he dropped his pack, whirled around and raised his gun. Mark and Penny scrambled up the rocks as another wild pig rushed at them with terrible speed.

David fired, but his shot was hurried and he missed. Just as the wild animal was on him, he aimed below the snarling jaws of the rushing beast and fired again. The heavy bullet knocked the charging animal backwards, just four feet from David's legs.

"Hurry, David!" Penny cried. "Hurry!" She and Mark had already climbed a dozen feet up the inclined rock formation. Mark had his gun aimed towards the jungle, his elbows braced on his knees. Blood was running down his face, but his hands were steady on the gun.

David turned, grabbed his pack, and holstered his gun as he ran and climbed desperately up the steep rocks. Mark's gun boomed once, then again, before David reached the ledge where they were sitting. He scrambled to a place beside Penny, turned, and looked back.

Another wild pig lay dead on the ground. Then others rushed out from the brush and milled around their dead comrades, sniffing the young peoples' scent and grunting with deadly anger. Both boys reloaded their guns at once.

"We'd better keep going," David said, rising wearily and picking up his pack. He led them up the sloping rock formation, spurred by the wild sounds from the animals below. The climb was not difficult, but it was steep enough to keep the pigs from following them, steep enough that they had to use their hands to help them climb.

As the three of them crawled carefully up the uneven gray rocks, David noticed a gap to their left and headed toward it. Here they were able to stand and walk. Passing between tall rock formations they found themselves in a flattened, circular area like an amphitheater. Rocks hemmed them in on all sides, but the clearing was large.

"I'm exhausted!" Penny said suddenly, taking off her pack and plopping on the ground. "I don't know when I've been so tired."

But she jumped up with a cry. "Mark, I forgot! Let me look at your cut!" Mark stood patiently while she studied the cut on his head. Then she took medicine from her pack, cleaned the wound, and taped gauze over it.

"There," she said with satisfaction, resting her hands on his shoulder, "I think you'll do fine!" She smiled up at him.

Mark gave her a hug with his left arm. Then he and Penny sat down with David. All of them were weary.

The boys still held their pistols.

They were soaked with sweat and dead-tired—tired from the long chase on the river, tired from the fight with the crocodiles, tired from the chase by the wild pigs, tired from the fast uphill climb. They drank from their canteens.

"Don't drink it all," David cautioned. "We don't know how long we'll need water."

"But the helicopter will be here soon," Penny reminded him.

"It's not here yet," Mark said. "Let's just be careful until it arrives. Then we can drink all we want." He hugged her reassuringly. "Thanks for helping me up back there. I didn't know what had hit me."

"How will the helicopter find us?" Penny asked, her dark eyes troubled. She had a smudge on her cheek and dirt on her sweat-soaked clothes. David thought to himself that she looked discouraged, and he didn't blame her—that's just how he felt.

"It won't be hard," Mark answered confidently, looking at the sky. "We can hear Dad's plane, and we're not far from where he saw us. Let's shoot another flare to let him know we changed positions."

He took a flare from his pack and shot it into the sky. When his dad flew low over them, he fired another.

"Now he knows where we are," he said, "even if he doesn't know why we moved."

Mr. Daring waggled his wings as he flew by to show that he'd spotted them.

"Well, it won't matter to the helicopter," David added. "It can land here just as well as where those pigs jumped us—in fact, this clearing's got more room." Then he said something that encouraged them even more. "The wild pigs should keep those men from coming any closer to us!"

"You're right," Mark agreed. "But I don't know how they could get past the crocodiles. The sound of their shots never seemed to come closer. I think they turned back before they got to the beach."

"But we can't be sure," David said, "and we don't know that there aren't any wild pigs around this clearing. Let's keep on the lookout."

Penny and Mark nodded in agreement, and the three of them sat on a large boulder, facing different directions and watching for danger.

The jungle was silent now. Perhaps the sound of their pistols had scared away the birds and frightened the other animals. Tired as they were, they kept alert and watched the jungle on every side. Their sole link with safety and home was the drone of Daring's plane as it made wide circles above.

It took a long hour for the helicopter to come. When they heard the thumping sound of its engines and blades, they fired another flare into the air to mark their position. Soon they saw it directly overhead. They stood up and waved as the noisy machine began to descend.

When the craft touched down, they waited for the

giant blades to stop before they rushed to the open door. A soldier was about to jump out and help them but when Mark yelled "Wild pigs!" The soldier reconsidered, then waved them in, and slammed shut the door.

The engine roared and the helicopter lifted into the sky. They were safe at last!

CHAPTER 18

THE RETURN

Mark yelled to the soldier over the engine's roar in the vibrating helicopter. "We left our canoe on the beach. Can we go pick it up?"

"I'll ask the pilot," the soldier yelled back. He went forward and talked for a minute, then returned and motioned Mark forward. "He says for you to come up and show him where it is."

Mark scrambled forward and crouched between the two pilots. He directed them to the beach as the pilot swung the craft in a turn and put it on a new course. Soon they saw the water and the island in the middle.

"There it is!" Mark pointed. "Watch out for crocodiles!"

The pilot nodded. He swooped over the canoe, across the river and the island, then back in a wide turn. Crocodiles were visible on the far beach, tearing at carcasses, and sometimes at each other. But there were none on the beach with the canoe.

"They won't come near us with the engine and the blades going," the pilot yelled to Mark. "I'll land on the beach and we can tie the boat between the skids. Keep an eye on the river just in case." He called the corporal forward and gave him instructions.

The helicopter landed beside the canoe as wind from the blades scattered sand on all side. The soldier jumped out, followed by Mark and David.

Mark watched the beach with gun drawn while David and the corporal dragged the canoe beneath the helicopter. They tied ropes under the bottom and through the front and back seats, drawing them taut. Mark's dad flew above them while they secured the canoe. Then they jumped back inside and the pilot lifted off, the canoe riding easily between the landing skids. The Cessna followed them to the ferry landing.

Here the pilot landed carefully, easing the helicopter with its low-slung canoe onto the grass of the small airstrip. The corporal helped the boys untie the boat and lower it to the ground.

"Many thanks!" Daring called to the pilot and the soldier. The men waved back as the helicopter lifted, swirled off in a graceful curve, and headed for its base.

"Oh, Daddy!" Penny cried joyfully as she threw her arms around his neck and felt his strong grip hold her close.

"Honey, I was sick with worry when I didn't find you on the river!" he said.

Mark said, "It's a wild story, Dad! It was Hoffmann and Walther—the guys you showed us at the airport— they tried to capture us!"

"Let's head for home before your mother gets worried," Daring said. "We'll talk later."

"Let's take the canoe to the ferry office," Mark told David. "The motorboat's scheduled to return it to Dr. Hawkins tomorrow. Do you see any damage?" he asked anxiously.

He and David looked it over with care. "None at all," David said. "Just some scrapes. These things are tough!"

"Still, we'll tell Dr. Hawkins what happened, and offer to pay for any repair," Mark replied. The boys lifted the light canoe and carried it to the office of the ferry manager.

There the manager promised to lock it up for the night and transfer it to the regular boat for return the next morning, just as they'd planned all along.

Mr. Daring thanked him and they headed for the plane.

"Let's get you kids home," Daring said with his arm around Penny. "What a time you've had!" He was shaken to realize the danger they'd been in. "Ride up front with me, Mark," he said as they got to the plane, "and tell me all about it."

Penny got in back, followed by David, and Mark and his father got in front. In a few minutes they had taken off and were flying home.

"I don't know why I'm so depressed all of a sudden," Penny said to David. "I should be happy that we're all safe." She leaned her head on his shoulder and closed her eyes.

"You're exhausted, that's why," David told her.

"We all are. See if you can't sleep on the way home."
He put his arm around her.

Mark told his dad of the events on the river and in
the jungle. His voice was barely distinguishable above
the noise of the engine. Soon, Penny was fast asleep.

Half an hour later, Mark looked back, saw Penny
asleep on David's shoulder, and gave his friend a big
wink. David grinned back, his face turning red.

All too soon for David's liking, the Cessna circled
over the home field and came in to land. Penny woke
and smiled up at David, but she didn't move her head
from his shoulder until the plane had stopped.

The whole family met them. Carolyn Daring had
heard the radio reports. She hugged the three young
folks, and then took Penny, Ruth, and Benjamin home
in her car while Mr. Daring and the boys went to the
office. There he had them tape record an account of
the day's encounter with the four men.

"Remember every detail you can," he said,
"because you'll forget a lot by morning." While they
were recording, Colonel Lamumba called.

"Good news, boys!" Daring said as he hung up the
phone. "The colonel's men caught the Land Rover!
Only two men were in it, however—Walther and an
African named Kala—and they won't say where
Hoffmann and the other one are. But that's half of
them! The colonel is elated! This breaks up the gang
behind the attacks on the mining industry here, and he
can hardly contain himself. There's a general alert out

for the two that are still loose."

He looked at the boys. "You two have done more than you realize!"

"Actually, Dad, we were just trying to get away!" Mark reminded him.

"Don't forget, Mr. Daring, it was Penny who spotted them waiting for us on the river," David added.

"I'll remember that, David, but you boys did what you've been trained to do—you got her safely away! That's why we've made you two work out and learn to fight and shoot—so you can do what Nehemiah told the Jewish men to do when they and their families were threatened with attack."

He turned and picked up his Bible from the desk. Turning to the fourth chapter of Nehemiah, he read verse 14: "'Don't be afraid of them. Remember the Lord, who is great and awesome, and fight for your brothers, your sons and your daughters, your wives and your homes.'" He looked up at the two young men. "That's what you've been trained to do, and that's what you've done. And I'm proud of you both!"

"Dad, I wish you could have seen Penny! She had to be scared when those men were chasing us—we were—and even more terrified when the crocodiles attacked. And then the wild pigs! But she did exactly what had to be done. And she never stopped paddling when David and I had to shoot. You would have been so proud to see her today!"

David spoke up. "Even when the wild pig was

attacking and Mark was on the ground, she ran to help him get up."

"I'm very proud of all of you," Daring replied.

Just then his phone rang again. He picked it up, answered, then handed it to Mark. "It's Benjamin. He wants to talk to you." Both boys had just slumped back in their seats, absolutely bushed. But Mark sat up and took the phone from his dad.

"Hi, Benjamin," he said. He listened for a minute, then hesitated, and looked up at David. "Well, uh, I guess we can—for a little while. We'll be there in a few minutes." He sighed and handed the phone back to his dad.

"Ruth and Benjamin want us to play in the pool. He reminded me that we promised to play with them when we got back." His shoulders sagged with the accumulated fatigue of their strenuous day; then he grinned at David. "I said we'd come."

Daring laughed. "Welcome to family life, boys! The day never ends!"

"I'll drive you up to the house." Daring laughed again, clapping them on the shoulders as they left the office. Fifteen minutes later Mark and David were chasing the little ones in the pool, whooping and laughing as if they'd just gotten up from a long nap!

CHAPTER 19

TO CAIRO!

David thought his watch had stopped. He'd just awakened, and the hour hand pointed to eleven o'clock! He knew that couldn't be right. Mark was still asleep—but the sun was shining through the curtains of the window.

Puzzled, David got out of bed and picked up Mark's watch from the bedside table. It also said eleven! Finally it dawned on him, the Darings must have let them sleep late after their adventures on the river. He stretched, dressed, and wandered into the kitchen. There he found Penny and her mom. Penny was wearing a pretty light blue bathrobe, and her eyes sparkled when she saw him.

"You lazy bones!" Penny scolded, smiling brightly. "Do you know what a sluggard is?"

"Nope, I just know where the orange juice is." He helped himself from the refrigerator.

Mrs. Daring laughed and asked, "What would you like, David, breakfast or lunch?"

David pondered her question while he drained the tall glass and then replied, "I think I'd like breakfast, if it's not too late."

"Not at all," Mrs. Daring said and began to heat

muffins and cook eggs while David sat down at the table with Penny. "Be honest, Penny," her mom continued, "and tell him when you got up."

"Oh, about 5 A.M.," Penny said with a straight face.

Her mom laughed and shook her head. "It was more like ten minutes ago. I wondered if you people would ever wake up! Is Mark still asleep?"

"Yes, ma'am, he is. I've tried to set him an example of diligence and early rising, but I'm afraid it hasn't done much good." David stretched. "Boy, was that a great sleep! I feel like a new man already—or I will when I've had breakfast," he corrected hastily.

Penny and her mom bowed their heads with David as he thanked the Lord for his food.

Mark wandered in while David was eating. He chose lunch and started making a sandwich. They figured that they'd slept more than thirteen hours, and they all felt rested.

The phone rang as the boys were eating. When Mrs. Daring picked it up, it was her husband. "Hi, Jim, they finally woke up." She listened for a moment. "Paul Froede! That's wonderful! Bring him along and we'll give him lunch."

"Mr. Froede—I thought he was in Cairo," Mark said.

"He just got in this morning. And he's leaving tomorrow. Your father's all excited because the project they're working on in Egypt has finally been approved by the government."

Penny looked over at David. "Mr. Froede's a great

friend and lots of fun. He and his wife have asked Mark and me to visit them in Cairo. They've promised to show us the pyramids and all kinds of ancient temples. But we haven't been able to go yet." She gave her mom a meaningful stare.

Mrs. Daring laughed. "All in good time, Penny— maybe sooner than you think! Go get dressed now so you can help me with lunch."

"What do you mean, 'sooner than you think'? What's up, Mom?" Penny asked, suddenly excited

"Hurry and get dressed and you'll find out "

Penny jumped up, glanced quickly at her brother with a questioning look in her eyes, and hurried to her room.

Mark was very alert. "What's going on, Mom?"

"I'll let your father tell you," she said. "Why don't you two go meet him."

"We're on our way!" Mark said jumping up. They left the house and walked down the drive, heading for the office building.

But almost immediately they saw Mr. Daring walking toward them. He was accompanied by a lean and powerfully built man with an athletic spring to his step. "That's Mr. Froede," Mark said to David.

Mark shook hands eagerly with the visitor. Daring introduced David. "This is the young man I told you about, Paul. What do you think?"

Paul Froede's bright blue eyes looked David over with a piercing yet friendly gaze. "He looks fine to me,

Jim. If you vouch for him, it's a deal."

Mark and David were flabbergasted. "What's the deal?" Mark asked.

His father laughed at their puzzled expressions. "Come inside, you two." He ran up the steps with his friend, and the boys hurried after them.

David whispered to Mark as they entered the kitchen. "What did he mean when he asked Mr. Froede what he thought of me?"

"I don't have any idea," Mark replied, "but I know Dad. He's got something up his sleeve!"

Mrs. Daring greeted Mr. Froede as an old friend. "Give me ten minutes, and I'll have something for you men to eat."

The men sat in the living room and talked about the diamond field Daring had just discovered. Mark and David were dying to learn what they had in mind, but neither Daring nor Mr. Froede mentioned it. Finally, Mrs. Daring called them in to eat.

Mr. Froede gave Penny a big hug when she joined them. The three teens weren't hungry since they'd just had breakfast, but they sat down with the others. After the blessing, Mrs. Daring asked, "What brings you here so suddenly, Paul?"

Froede waved his fork. "What brought me here was a sudden longing I had to see you and Jim and all these kids of yours! And to meet this young man." He nodded at David and grinned. David grinned back, more puzzled than ever.

"Wait a minute, you storyteller!" She laughed. "I know your mother was Irish. Are you giving me some blarney?"

Froede and her husband grinned. "Actually, Carolyn," Froede answered, "we've got a real opportunity in Cairo and I need Jim's help—and maybe some of his team." Again he waved his fork in a broad gesture that seemed to include Mark, David, and Penny.

She laughed at his evasiveness. "Let's hear it then."

"Let me tell you what's happened," Froede said eagerly. He began to describe an elaborate building project he and Daring had become involved in several years before. There had been delays, however, because of government restrictions. The building their clients had planned turned out to be right over an ancient tomb. Such sites were protected by severe laws. And their locations had to be kept secret, to keep out plunderers.

"But my translator just left me!" Paul Froede cried, waving his fork again. "The girl he's been pursuing for three years suddenly lost her senses and agreed to marry him—at once! He flew back to Paris two days ago." He groaned. "And just when I needed him the most. You see, the firm we're working for is jointly owned by French and German companies. We deal with their people, and we deal with their documents. We've got to have someone who knows both those languages."

Mr. Daring broke in. "That's why he came here, Carolyn. Mark and Penny know French, and David knows German."

Penny and Mark were flabbergasted. Mrs. Daring smiled at their excitement.

"You mean we can go with you to Cairo, Uncle Paul?" Penny asked.

"If your parents will lend you to me for a few weeks, I could really use you!" he replied with a broad grin.

"And David can go too?" she asked quickly.

"If he's willing and his parents agree. I need people who know French and people who know German—and he knows German!"

"David," Daring said, "I've already called your parents. They say it's a great idea. I told them you'd call them in a little while."

"Gosh, Mr. Daring! Thanks!"

"Wow!" Mark exclaimed. "Egypt!"

"Pyramids! And temples!" Penny added, her eyes shining.

Paul Froede looked at the two boys. "If my company pays for your flight and work, then I expect to get my money's worth out of you—understand?" He tried to appear stern, then spoiled the effect by winking at Penny. She laughed back.

"Yes, sir!" the boys answered at once.

The afternoon was spent in frenzied planning and packing. Again and again Mrs. Daring told Penny, "You won't have room for all those clothes!" Finally, just after dinner, their bags were ready. Paul Froede had their parents and little Ruthie and Benjamin in stitches with some story when the three came into the living room.

"We're going for a walk, Dad," Mark said.

"Don't stay too late," their father advised. "You leave with Mr. Froede early in the morning." Froede winked at them.

The three walked down the drive from the house, past the labs and offices. The moon shed a magic haze, and they were surrounded by the sounds of insects and the scents of wild flowers.

Penny walked between the boys, still wearing the skirt and blouse she'd put on for dinner. "You look great!" David had said, as he held her chair for her at the table. Both families had raised their sons to do this, but until this evening Mark had taken pleasure in edging David out.

The adventures of the day before had drawn the three friends even closer than they'd been already. They all felt this new sense of comradery as they strolled down the drive.

"Boy," David said, "you folks live in the fast lane, all right! I thought I was going to have a vacation here!"

"Actually, David," Mark protested, "these last days have not been normal—I've told you that. Our lives are usually quiet and peaceful. Aren't they, Penny?"

"We sure do! That's why I'm surprised we invited such an action-oriented guy to visit us! Why, he's rushed us through danger after danger ever since he got here! No wonder his folks let him come—they must need a rest!"

"Wait a minute," David protested, "I'm the quiet one. I just like to relax. You people live as if you're packing ten days into one. You'll burn yourselves out before you reach twenty!"

They argued amiably as they walked in the moonlight, then turned reluctantly back to the house, not wanting the pleasant evening to end. But then they thought of flying to Cairo with Mr. Froede! What new adventures awaited them there?